PENGUIN BOOKS

CHICKPEAS TO COOK & OTHER STORIES

Nilanjana Sengupta is an author based in Singapore. Her last publication was *The Votive Pen: Writings on Edwin Thumboo* (Penguin Random House SEA, 2020), shortlisted for both the Singapore Literature Prize 2022 and Singapore Book Awards 2021. Her other books include *A Gentleman's Word: The Legacy of Subhas Chandra Bose in Southeast Asia* (ISEAS-Yusof Ishak Institute, 2012), *The Female Voice of Myanmar: Khin Myo Chit to Aung San Suu Kyi* (Cambridge University Press, 2015), *Singapore, My Country: Biography of M Bala Subramanian* (World Scientific Press, 2016). Sengupta also writes for *The Straits Times* and for publications of the National Heritage Board, Singapore. Her books have been critically acclaimed, adopted for university courses and translated into multiple languages. She has been associated with the ISEAS-Yusof Ishak Institute as well as NUS in various research capacities.

T0148810

ADVANCE PRAISE FOR *CHICKPEAS TO COOK &* *OTHER STORIES*

Chickpeas To Cook shines with insight and humanity. It opens our eyes to the beauty of the faith and beliefs that sustain the small minority communities in Singapore. The rich narrative sections show how individuals live out this faith in their daily lives, and how resilient wives and mothers try to pass on the values and traditions that preserve the community's distinctive identity within the multi-ethnic multi-religious island nation. I have enjoyed and learned from this book. Thank you, Nilanjana Sengupta.

—Suchen Christine Lim, Author

While the non-fiction passages are informative, focusing on some of Singapore's smallest and most often overlooked, communities, it was the voices of the women within them that made them come alive for me. Narrating their stories via conversations, letters, dialogues and in prose, they made me feel like a best friend was laying bare her heart to me. And unexpected, perhaps—considering their very different religious and cultural backgrounds—is how similar their very different struggles towards identity felt.

—Ovidia Yu, Author

Chickpeas to Cook is more than a book; it is a mansion. Nilanjana Sengupta sets out to house many splendid ideas and, first and foremost, pays homage to friendship. Her inherently self-renewing work soars as gorgeous writing inscribing a single sacred truth: every friend is another life and another heart you have.

—Gwee Li Sui, Poet, Graphic Artist, Literary Critic

Small communities must remain orthodox to retain their identity, drawing energy from the past to survive. This insightful book explores both the strengths and the limitations this imposes on individuals, especially women, who wish to expand their horizons and step into the modern age. Nilanjana Sengupta admirably captures the paradoxes such communities face and the difficult life journeys of those caught between the past and the future. This is a valuable work that brings into perspective the human side of communities that are often overlooked.

—Dr Meira Chand, Author

I need to let my mind leave its incisive nature and my heart its desirous pursuits unveiling *Chickpeas to Cook*. I have to remind myself that there is so much tenderness, unchartered feelings, and mysteries as I lift the veils of faith, culture, community, and gender that are richly and sensitively presented by Nilanjana Sengupta in the stories. There is an initial desire for me as a reader to find common grounds between the stories, but I decide not to let my heart, mind, and soul be reduced and fenced by it. The book is just so layered and faceted that it is best to let the light that emanates from its pages lead the reader to its wisdom and surprise, wherever that might be. The feeling after completing it is of joyful shyness, just like the moment of unveiling of the bride by the groom on their first matrimonial night. That is strange, because such a feeling is normally felt in the beginning, but perhaps that is just it, this book teases the reader further with a new smile.

—Isa Kamari, Author

Focusing on women from Singapore's lesser known, and somewhat invisible, religious communities, *Chickpeas to Cook* conveys the intricacies, aesthetics, and elegance of their everyday lives in the island's multi-ethnic and multireligious landscape. The book presents a poignant tapestry of women's seemingly ordinary practices, sentiments, and philosophies, which sustain families and build communal solidarities through a commitment to the values of empathy, integrity, determination and resilience.

—Dr Vineeta Sinha, Deputy Head,
Department of Sociology, National University of Singapore

Sengupta's *Chickpeas to Cook* is different from all the books on religion I have read. This is gourmet stuff, cooked by an outstanding wordsmith with a spellbinding storytelling talent that kept me turning the pages to consume with delight every single page. I find myself inspired by the inner beauty of religious humanitarianism practised in simplicity by the women in the stories. I can only echo John Newton's famous line, 'I was blind but now I see.'

—William Tan, Head of Singapore
Kindness Movement

I have had the pleasure of accompanying the author on several of her literary journeys. These have yielded much acclaimed books including *A Gentleman's Word*, *The Female Voice of Myanmar*, and *A Votive Pen*. In *Chickpeas to Cook*, Nilanjana has excelled herself by dealing with two sensitive topics—religion and the position of women of smaller communities in Singapore. As a person actively involved in the promotion of inter-faith dialogue, I am particularly impressed by the snapshots of the various religions that make up the tapestry of the religious landscape of Singapore.

—K. Kesavapany, Past President,
Inter-Religious Organisation (IRO)

Chickpeas to Cook & Other Stories

Nilanjana Sengupta

PENGUIN BOOKS

An imprint of Penguin Random House

PENGUIN BOOKS

USA | Canada | UK | Ireland | Australia
New Zealand | India | South Africa | China | Southeast Asia

Penguin Books is part of the Penguin Random House group of companies
whose addresses can be found at global.penguinrandomhouse.com

Published by Penguin Random House SEA Pte Ltd
9, Changi South Street 3, Level 08-01,
Singapore 486361

First published in Penguin Books by Penguin Random House SEA 2022
Copyright © Nilanjana Sengupta 2022

10 9 8 7 6 5 4 3 2 1

The views and opinions expressed in this book are the author's own and the
facts are as reported by her which have been verified to the extent possible,
and the publishers are not in any way liable for the same.

ISBN 9789815017038

Typeset in Adobe Garamond Pro by MAP Systems, Bangalore, India

www.penguin.sg

A chickpea leaps almost over the rim of the pot where it's being boiled
'Why are you doing this to me?'

—*Rumi*

My shire

CONTENTS

AUTHOR'S NOTE

A chickpea speaks . . .

I think I was around six when one day, as we often did, we went to the temple on the outskirts of our city. We reached early. The river flowing alongside the temple was yet to awaken, the still dark sky was heavy with the promise of dawn. Inside, it was cast in pitch-black shadows, a few worshippers shrouded in white sat in solemn meditation. At the far end of the cavernous hall, the priest with one sinewy arm raised aloft a heavy brass lamp while with another he rang the temple bell, and the morning service began. And yet, despite the velvety dark, the ringing did not rend through the night. It seemed to emerge instead from its very depths, carrying with it some of the travails that the day would bring and an anguished need to surrender.

I sat as close to my mother as I possibly could, with my knee touching hers, and sensed her absolute stillness, as if all her energies were centred at a point which, for once, was not turned towards me. Glancing at her face, to my surprise, I noticed tears streaming down her cheeks. Was my mother, who ruled our household with an iron hand, weeping? It surprised me, but what surprised me more was that there were still some things that my six-year-old head couldn't wrap itself around. And then I turned and saw the look of entreaty on the face of the God, and, for a moment, the world stood still. It felt as though Him, my mother, and the darkly mysterious night crouching outside were all tied together in one vast cycle. A cycle in which the lamp and the bell left dancing, hologram-like shadows and my mother's tears softened with a wrenching poignancy, making sure I never forgot the moment; or the fact that it was exactly then that the first fingers of crimson touched the night sky.

So, does such a memory—or if I dare to call it a vision— make me a rarity? No, it does not. To many of us, such moments occur, particularly in early youth, particularly when our senses are heightened. They hold a hint of a revelation, what the Persian poets called a seed of light, when the chickpea leaps nearly to the rim. It is the kind of moment about which Wordsworth wrote, 'And I have felt a presence that disturbs me with the joy of elevated thoughts . . .' If one is ready to embark on a journey of self-annihilating love, of a denuding union with a vaster identity, then such moments can swing one out of the orbit of everyday life. Otherwise? Otherwise, the chickpea returns to the pot to be mixed with spices and rice so that it can be the 'lovely vitality of a human being'.

I, at six, was obviously not ready. In fact, as family annals go, I dozed off soon after and on waking, demanded to breakfast off the savoury and sweets that sold in the shops outside—catering to ardent devotees exactly like me. But with the passage of time, as I follow the meandering path, sometimes through forests of dusk-laden autumn trees, sometimes up a panting hill carrying the sun on my back, I feel the urge to return to such moments,

moments that carry in their heart reflections of perfection, myriad little lights that dance at the crests of a rippling ocean.

In *Chickpeas to Cook*, I explore the multi-religious, multicultural patina of Singapore, intentionally choosing the smallest of communities, sometimes no more than a few hundred families, to pique the interest of the post-Jobs, post-Mark, post-David (no, the references are not biblical) reader. It is a look at the collective subtext of the grand, graceful, wise tide of timeless religious humanism that flows at the heart of a city, hidden away by its cosmopolitan urbanism and a people known to possess a pragmatic, if politically accommodating, nature; brought out to be aired while curating exhibitions or during demographic surveys. It is about those numerous women who, after the day's work is done, sit for evening vespers and knowingly commit the certainty of their familiar selves to an uncertain, unknown alterity.

Yes, women are my central protagonists, women who with their daily tasks of cooking, sewing and bearing life plunge us into the immediacy of cosmic creativity; women who at times like Attar's nightingale pour out the pain of lovers note by note, and at times is the haughty, preening peacock carrying the beauty of paradise in her plumage. Their multiple universes overstep and interweave, making for a glorious constellation of shared living—helpers who just can't get it right, parents who decide to fall ill just when one is sinking into pre-menopausal depression, and the wretched new expats who come in to destroy order and sanctity. Each is a spark scattered on a graph towards enlightenment, together they are a country in intimate communion with itself—no, not to transcend reality, but merely to embrace it more fully.

As I've progressed from one faith to another, maybe my questions have sharpened, my realizations have taken on a more profound note. This of course has nothing to do with the subject, but as Paulo Coelho said, once I had the answers, the questions changed. For the religious element, I return to my six-year-old self, cleaving through layers of ritual and texts and doctrines to the foundational bedrock where religion is merely a path guided by love to know your higher self, in short, the path of a mystic. It is as elementary as a McDonald's fry, as ancient as Philo when he said, it is a direct personal communion of a soul that no longer reasons but feels and knows. For my understanding of difficult facts, I lean heavily on Andrew Harvey, the scholar of mystic traditions, a clutch of Persian poems, some beautiful calligraphic scrolls (Arabic in Jali Diwani and Chinese in Xing scripts), and a woman's instinct—which despite what my husband maintains, I know to be unfailing!

And lastly, before I conclude, in this book I have been aware that I cross boundaries, walk the holy ground of other cultures. I have tried to tread as cautiously as possible, listening closely to interviews, depending extensively on mainstream scriptures, but if inadvertent flaws and follies remain, may the blame come to me while the merit is shared by all.

Nilanjana Sengupta
Kew Crescent, Singapore

ISLAM

al-Nur, *Qur'an 24:35*

the lamp is in a glass,
the glass as it were a glittering star—
lit from a blessed olive tree

Islam

The essence of Islam, derived from the Arabic root s-l-m, is peace and surrender, a peace that comes from an unquestioning submission to the power of God. This quality of passionate humility comes from the Qur'an, ablaze as it is with awe and wonder at the glory of Allah. It inspires an exquisite courtesy of the soul and a reverence towards the universe as is evident in the best traditions of Islamic mysticism.

Dawoodi Bohras

The Dawoodi Bohra community in Singapore is around 800 families strong, with the first migrants having come in the mid-1880s. Though they trace their roots back to Egypt and Yemen, the immediate port of call is Surat on the western coast of India where, long back, Hindu traders were converted by Muslim missionaries. Even today, older community members in Singapore recall mothers wearing a *bindi*[1] on their forehead or Deepavali lamps being lit in their homes. Besides English or any of the local languages, their native tongue is the *Lisan al-Dawat*, an interesting combination of sharp, peppery Gujarati sounds and more sonorous Arabic or Urdu words. Essentially traders and businessmen, the community, by choice, is apolitical, willing to go with the government of the day.

As Shi'a Muslims, the Battle of Karbala forms the nesting myth of the community, an important symbol of resistance against tyranny for all those who suffer injustice. The compassion with which Hussain ibn Ali treated his foes even as his family

---

[1] The dot in the middle of the forehead Indian women apply to beautify themselves.

was decimated remains a poignant narrative of faith against all adversity. And therefore, with a woman's usual perspicuity, an interviewee comments, 'Our fate is naught but love.' Consequently, the ten days of Muharram, commemorating the anniversary of the Battle of Karbala, are the main annual event. Celebrated in the first month of the Muslim calendar, it sets the tone for the rest of the year, lending to their faith a votive colour of sacrificial devotion.

Interesting is the special place women hold in this social milieu of entrepreneurs and traders. Here too, it is the Battle of Karbala which forms the fountainhead. Replete with stories of Khadeejah, Zainab, and the young, gentle Sakeenah, the bloody battlefields witnessed spectacular transformation of role for these women. Thus, there is Zainab—from 'sufferer' and 'bystander' to 'Zainab the Lionheart' in the aftermath of battle, the one to disseminate Hussain's message of compassion and unquestioning faith. 'Our Syedna[2] speaks a great deal about these women,' an interviewee mentions, and by doing so, women are encouraged to be less sentimental and more agentive.

Incidentally, early marriage is encouraged for the women of this community which traces descent from the Fatimid Caliphate, a dynasty that continues the bloodline of Fatimah, Prophet Muhammad's daughter. But—as the women hasten to add—this is irrespective of gender and there is equal emphasis on education. Thus, for the Bohris, the mausoleum of the sovereign queen of Yemen, Hurrat-ul Malika, who ruled over the royal court with her face unveiled, remains an important pilgrimage; and practices such as that of community kitchens (*Faiz-ul Mawaid Burhaniyah* or FMB) have been instituted with the express purpose of allowing women freedom from

---

[2] Religious leader of the Bohris.

household chores. 'Our women are allowed to look pretty,' they say, and pretty they are in their colourful *ridahs*[3] designed with lace, embroidery, and crochet work.

Of course, in the present times, it is a changing world that they have to contend with. A changing world where, on days of high alert, a young Bohri man carrying a haversack might very well be stopped at MRT stations for security check or when notions of fake news and fundamentalist possibilities of leveraging the social media are increasingly topics of concern. A woman confides, 'When I first started my course in Singapore Open University, others wouldn't sit beside me.' Fortunately, though, she could dispel her cohort's bias when she won a gold medal and made it to the newspapers!

The Syedna has tried to respond to this by pulling the community closer and carving out a distinct identity for it, away from mainstream Muslim culture. Whereas until the 1980s, wearing a ridah was not compulsory, more stringent norms of attire have been put in place since then. There is also the increasing popularity of the four Jamea schools (in Surat, Mumbai, Karachi, and Nairobi), community-run Dawoodi Bohra religious institutions which also embrace and teach secular world views. Young *mumins* and *mumineens* or male and female scholars might enter such a school at the age of fourteen and spend the next eleven years there, passing out with what is equivalent to a post-graduate degree. The community's attempt remains to continuously move closer to the basics, be it in terms of food conservation and environmental awareness or teaching youngsters to differentiate between *zahir* and *batin* or what we call external and internal interpretations of the Holy Qur'an. It is a balance of internal and external lives, *rozi*[4] and religion

---

[3] The two-piece attire that a Bohri woman wears, along with a headscarf.
[4] Profession

that the Bohris seek, none being sufficiently fulfilling without the other.

In Singapore, the Burhani Masjid next to the Chinese Chamber of Commerce is the pivot around which religious and cultural life revolves. The pastor or *amil sahib* leads the namaz and is the de facto community leader while the mosque has the customary *jamaat khaana* where the faithful gather for after-prayer meals, particularly Friday dinners. The religious epicentre, though, lies in Mumbai, the residence of the fifty-third and current Da'i of Dawoodi Bohras, Syedna Mufaddal Saifuddin. If among Singapore residents, there is some jealous longing for the bustling Bhendi Bazaar, the original home of the Bohris where the puff pastry sweetmeat *malai nu khajlu* sells at streetside stalls and the latest ridah-fashion prevails, then it is quickly brushed aside.

* * *

Ablaze

There was a desperation to my footsteps that day as I entered the home of one who I call my 'mita[5] or 'friend of surrender'. Despite the obvious kindness of the community and my tedious study, my thoughts on the Bohri Muslims just didn't seem to come together. The answers lay out of bounds, like the great Bohri thaal[6] *that stood against the patio wall, half-hidden behind a cupboard, gleaming with a dull lustre.*

Then she walked in, rather, sparkled towards me, and I noted a strange contrariness to her, a disarming docility while she spoke to me and a startling regality when she interacted with her family.

---

[5] The word means 'friend' in Pali, from the Sanskrit, Mitra.

[6] The large metal dish around which eight to nine people sit to dine as part of the Bohri tradition of communal dining.

*Was it just the insider/outsider thing, I wondered? But then, I noticed
her talk to Nooriya, her daughter, and I realized that it was a hard-
earned status. It came not from the social power of a matriarch
but from an unusual alchemy of emotions born of long days and
nights of introspection and self-questioning, from looking at life in
all its harrowing failures, from walking a path that grows gradually
luminous even as all doors close, from working out some answers for
yourself and knowing them to be true only because they are.*

*Here I have changed names for the sake of privacy. I have also
compressed into a single visit a story that emerged bit by bit as I got
to know Sakinah better for no other reason but to convey the richness
and intensity of the patina of Bohri life.*

At that time, my friend Sakinah lived just off Marine Cres, in a
block where the bus entered a quiet loop of a feeder route. And I
left my home every afternoon in search of stories, the one activity
that could draw me away from my studious routine, when I'd
walk around observing how the people of this great metropolis
lived till it became an almost intuitive habit, noting external
details but attempting to pole-vault straight into the soul.

And so, I walked across a park where children played under
a *ketapang* tree which sheds crimson leaves in autumn, and the
walls were graffitied with stories of community living. At the
sound of my footsteps, geckos skittered, rustling into alcoves
of darkness.

I had been to this little ground-floor apartment before,
watched my friend as she was torn in a thousand different
directions, trying to single-handedly put together her daughter
Nooriya's wedding. Now, too, there was the steel thaal, rolled
away to a corner, a reminder of Nooriya's engagement. It stood

half-hidden behind a cupboard, reflecting the dull gleam of an overcast sky.

The long sliver of the drawing room stood in its usual quivering, regimented order. There was the single glass column of travel memorabilia with gold trimmings on top like the *juloos*[7] decorations of Muharram when mourners file past in silence, dressed in funereal black. There was the faux Persian rug under my feet through which ran a thread of glittery gold. On one of the whitewashed walls hung a large portrait of the Syedna, his face peaceful, numinous; on the other, a painting of the bloodied fields of Karbala, the sky hanging low, smouldering, the last star-bursts of battle still visible.

Sakinah walked in and, as always, I was struck by the strange, shuddering vitality she embodied, as if some power had breathed a life into her that was different from my own. Her hair fell in thick, unruly cascades, her long silk kaftan came to a demure, swishing halt at her feet and yet its motif of tiger lilies seemed to bloom with a primal energy all its own, stark against the velvety green background. Her toenails, like other Muslim women's, were painted with henna and yet the ankles her kaftan revealed were sturdy, well-worked. And though she extended a polite hand in greeting, when I looked into her eyes, I felt swallowed by a fire, the same fierce, thrashing desire that pushed and drove her, lent a stubborn vigour to her flying feet. It was as strong and undeniable as birthing pangs and it seemed to split her into two.

At this point, she met my eyes squarely and cried, 'He'd say, "When they bury me in Choa Chu Kang,[8] I'll make sure you are buried under me!" Imagine!'

---

[7] Reference to the decorations of the Tazia processions of Muharram.
[8] Location of Muslim cemetery in Singapore.

Her tone indicated that her mind had not lost track of what we had talked about the last time we met. I sat down on the carpet to listen to her. The afternoon sun was blazing again, lighting up the green walls of the room behind her with a magical jungle luminescence. In the kitchen, Nooriya was heating up a plate of *varkhi* samosas.[9] The microwave made a tame beeping sound, entirely out of place in this house.

'It was Nooriya who warned me,' she said. She looked surprised, even after all these years. 'That little chit of a girl, turning around and telling me, "Mummy, run away, run away from here, it's all so dirty!" But I didn't listen to her, you know. I'd slap her instead and scream, "Is this how I've taught you to respect your elders and betters?"'

Her daughter wouldn't reply. She'd go to her room, quietly lock the door against all predators. And then, late in the evening, when Farad returned from his shop bearing a box of curry puffs, he'd go up to her door and beg, 'Come out, my *jaan*,[10] come out *dikhra*,[11] see what I've got for you!'

But the door remained obstinately shut and Sakinah and Farad would silently nod at each other in mutual understanding. These adolescent girls!

'Soda water!' Farad would mouth, winking, and Sakinah would smile, already turning back to her cooking. Tomorrow, Nooriya had early-morning school . . . why did Amma look so sad nowadays . . . oh, she shouldn't forget, the curtains needed to be put into the washing machine, she would have to soak them in Clorox tonight. Her mind would churn out the litany.

---

[9] Meat-filled samosas, typically Bohri.
[10] Heart or soul, lifeforce.
[11] Gujarati term of endearment.

'If only, if only, if only,' Sakinah sighs. 'If only Abba had not been so proud, if only Amma hadn't cried so much,' she makes a defeated, rueful gesture at everything that lies around her in the room, 'all of this wouldn't have happened.'

For the moment, she looks nothing like herself. The light in her eyes is snuffed out; I find myself gazing into pools of darkness.

Sakinah was born when this city looked very different. They lived in Geylang wherein nested their little Bohri neighbourhood—Lorong Challis. The houses were around a single courtyard, residence of the original Surtis of Gujarat. They were the *apnawaalas*[12] here, the insiders, of one flock, where every woman was an aunt whose home you could walk into for a cup of chai. Down the road was Queen's Theatre where they went to watch Malay romances. It was rumoured that ghosts[13] from the past could very well appear and sit on the chair next to you and it was common for truant sons to exclaim when caught by their fathers, 'But Abba, you saw a ghost, that wasn't me, I was home all evening, studying for my exam,' with their mothers nodding in eager acquiescence.

And in Lorong Challis, Sakinah's Abba was a hero, the local Robin Hood who wore thick gold chains around his neck and had his Brylcreemed hair brushed into a puff. And in the basement of their house, after climbing down a short flight of stairs, was their kitchen where her Amma spent most of her days, sometimes even parts of the nights.

---

[12] A Bohri term meaning the insiders of the community, a concept like the thaal, emphasizing their love of community bond.

[13] Stories of ghosts abound because the theatre was built on a cemetery.

I watch Sakinah's eyes cloud over as she recalls. The kitchen where it remained cool even on the hottest of summer days, where on rainy days the moisture rose through the flagstones so the floor was always slightly damp under your feet.

'Have you ever touched mould before?' she asks, extending her fingers as if she can feel it even now. 'It feels strange, you know, when the plaster crumbles, as though the very walls are giving way.'

It was here that Amma would sit hunched over her little hand-pumped stove, rolling out parathas with a rolling pin. Her arms would move, making her glass bangles tinkle, and Sakinah and her elder sister would sit by her, playing with their abacus. The wooden beads of the abacus would fall, one after the other—click, click, click—into the silence.

On one such evening when the fire cast long, dancing shadows on the wall, Amma told them a story, the story of a queen whom the king wanted to kill so that he could escape her bewitching beauty. So, he sent his best men—the bravest knights and the most conniving ministers. And yet none could slay her. The queen merely smiled and the king, against his wishes, walked deeper into her snare.

Here, Amma stopped and looked at Sakinah and her sister. 'You know why no one could kill her?' she'd asked, pursing her lips, protracting the suspense. And then, looking at their upturned faces, revealed, 'Because the clever queen had hidden her jaan in a box, high up on a treetop, in the nest of a singing koel.'

'Where do you keep your jaan, Amma?' Sakinah asked, wide-eyed.

Amma burst out laughing, looked around at the kitchen, at the dancing shadows, the fireflies escaping from the stove. 'Here . . . somewhere,' she said mysteriously.

Sakinah looked around fearfully. But Ben,[14] always cleverer than her, laughed at her confusion, 'She means us, you dodo. She means us. Her jaan is inside us.'

I watch Sakinah get up and pace around restlessly. She takes long, manly strides and the room with its lace doilies and trimmed table cloth suddenly seems too small for her.

'But he would never leave us in peace,' she flings at me. 'Never! He would come down the stairs, and from Abba's footsteps we would know what kind of a mood he was in.'

If, along with Abba, there was the sound of other footsteps, they would know they were safe, at least for the time being, till the guests left. But if he was alone, Amma would silently meet their eyes over the fire, and they'd know it was time to put away the toys. For no one knew when Abba's hands, always restless, would hover over his belt.

But that day, they did not hear Abba's footsteps. When Sakinah peered at the sound of voices outside the kitchen door, she knew why—that night, Abba was being carried downstairs on the shoulder of his friends. His friends had milled around him, and the loud cheering had hit the rafters of the basement, boomed in their tiny kitchen till it reverberated back from the trembling walls.

'Long live Hasan Bhai! Hasan Bhai zindabad!' his friends had cried.

They'd talked about the task Abba had accomplished that day—retrieving a man from a house of questionable morality. 'You should have seen the expression on the man's face when

---

[14] Gujarati term for sister.

Hasan Bhai dragged him to his wife—standing there, shivering, in nothing but his towel!' they had laughed.

Sakinah had sneaked a look at her father's face from under her lashes—that broad smile of satisfaction, indulgent, even benign; that proud twitch in his jawline as he surveyed his friends below him, holding him up. It was the look of a man who knows how much power he holds in his grasp, when he doesn't need to flex his muscles any longer.

She'd seen him that day, perched right up there, on top of the world, and known that's where she needed to keep him if she was to be happy.

I watch Sakinah turn the bangle on her hand over and over again. After a pause, she looks up, sighs, 'But who could explain all this to Amma?'

The day had been a long one for Amma, by then already into her third trimester. This pregnancy with Sakinah's younger sister was proving to be difficult. Her feet would swell up every day like pav.[15] The elderly *Kakijee*[16] next door had advised her to massage her feet with mustard oil every night. It was late; all she wanted was to go to bed. And so, when Abba told her to cook dinner for his friends, she looked at his face for a moment and, in a voice that hovered uncertainly between assertion and entreaty, whispered, '*Nai, me nai keru.*'[17]

Sakinah watched Abba slowly walk into the kitchen. He looked around with great deliberation at the paratha that lay half-rolled on the rolling board, the dry flour strewn on the floor like the talcum powder he liked to use. And then, in a flash, he

---

[15] Small bun-like bread.
[16] Aunt
[17] No, I won't.

had picked up the *chamchi*,[18] still hot from the flaming griddle, and slashed it across Amma's face.

'I didn't look up, I couldn't,' Sakinah says.

In the silence, she heard the beads of Ben's wooden abacus falling—click, click, click. Then, after a while, Amma started to cry softly, making a low mewling noise. And in her head, Sakinah knew *no* was not a word to use in front of Abba.

For a while, we sit in silence, unable to continue. It is Nooriya who distracts us. She has walked in with cups of chai and samosa. Not the blushing bride, she looks calm, her small frame held erect. She sets down the tray with an efficient clink, straightens the table cloth with a flick of her hand.

I see mother and daughter exchange a glance and almost in reflex action Sakinah pushes back her hair, straightens her back.

'My Nooriya will go to Paris after her wedding, you know. She's trained in linguistics, already learning French, so she can work there. *Voulez-Vous*, how do you say it, my jaan?' she laughs.

But Nooriya does not smile back, instead she leaves with a polite nod in my direction. Sakinah shakes her head behind her daughter's retreating back, 'So serious all the time! Relax, I keep telling her, enjoy your wedding. I remember I was so excited at the time of my marriage . . .'

She turns back to me, continues with her story.

'That evening, I saw Abba's pride and decided to make him proud myself. And so, I'd study hard and bring back a trophy from school every year and watch Abba stand there with his chest a little bit more puffed out, his gold chains sparkle a little bit more in the sun. People would say, proud daughter of proud father and Abba would smile . . .' She pauses again, the flash that I've always

---

[18] Spoon, ladle

associated with her is back in her eyes, though it doesn't take long for it to die down. She says in a morose undertone, 'But then, Amma could never understand, could she?'

It was yet another evening. It had rained heavily the entire day. By then she was in junior college. They had moved to Chai Chee, the first of the Housing & Development Board apartment buildings of Singapore. She'd known she was late and so had sprinted up the staircase and rang the doorbell. But the door hadn't opened. She'd rung again, but it had remained shut. Aunt Susan from next door had come out to plead for her. 'Come on, brother Hasan, have pity on the girl *lah*!'

Finally, when Abba opened the door a couple of hours later, Sakinah was soaked through. The street outside had quietened down. Without a word she'd entered, sat down for her dinner. But then, at the sight of her, Amma had started crying and she'd known—this is it.

Abba had screamed, '*Suk kam itni mori avi*? (Why did you come so late?)' and hit her hard across her face. He hit her again and again until Sakinah fell face forward into her food. And all the while, she could hear Amma cry, making the same soft, wailing sound that she always did, till Abba had taken his face close to Amma's and jeered, 'Soda water!'

'That day, I thought to myself, what kind of a love is this? Amma was crying because she loved me so much, Abba was hitting me because he wanted me to be a good girl, and yet why didn't their love make me happy?'

And so, she had jumped at his proposal when Farad entered her life, he with his roses, handmade cards, and gentle words of endearment. He seemed to be everything that Abba was not and yet, strangely enough, Abba had approved his soon-to-be son-in-law and, for once, Sakinah felt she was doing everything right.

I have bitten into a clove in the samosa, its sharp pungency fills my mouth. Sakinah sits on the sofa with her feet curled in under her as she recalls how Abba had been happy with her choice of groom.

'Rich *chokro se!*'[19] he had told his friends. 'Big family business.' And then, looking at Amma with a slightly ingratiating smile, 'Our girl has done us proud, *dikhri ye humari izzat rakhi.*'

Amma had turned away with her lips pursed, refusing to be drawn into the conversation. Sakinah had smiled to herself, enjoying her mother's singular moment of triumph. But inside, she was relieved, all the while knowing that she would leave home, never to return. Her *nikah* would be her grand escape.

The wedding ceremony was beyond anything Sakinah had ever dreamt of. Farad had made sure the whole community was invited to watch the spectacle, the pathway to his house was lined with a thick carpet of her favourite flower—red roses— for Sakinah to walk on.

But as it often happens, the moment you take life for granted, it takes an unruly turn. Thus, even while she and Amma prayed hard for everything to go well, Sakinah realized how intensely uncomfortable she was with her new in-law's home: the sparkly pink walls, the muddy green on the window panes that turned sunlight into sleaze, the oil paintings of nude women that adorned the walls and the way her father-in-law pointed them out to her, peered close to her face and asked if she liked them, as if genuinely interested in a connoisseur's opinion.

And then, there was Farad—a good eighteen years older than her, with a Burmese ruby on his index finger that shone with a secret light. He had decorated their wedding bed with white tube roses

---

[19] The boy is rich.

and waited for her amidst a mound of pillows on their wedding night. 'Jaan, I do hope you know how to keep a man happy,' he whispered and his hand, when he touched hers, felt clammy.

She'd tried to speak to Amma but her mother had been dismissive, 'Come on dikhra, don't be silly. That's how rich people live, that's how love is.'

But then Sakinah, didn't have too long to fret about it. Within the first year of her marriage, she was pregnant with Nooriya and as she dealt with morning sickness, cramps and fatigue, the small signs of discomfiture were pushed far away into dark corners.

It was only when Nooriya was much older that the first warning bells sounded.

That day, Farad had taken Nooriya to his shop and when they returned, her daughter wore a wan, pinched look. Sakinah noticed Farad trying to placate her. *'Kitni khoobsurat che, pari na jemaat!'*[20] he said, placing his hand on her head, but Nooriya merely pushed his hand away, locking herself in her room.

Sakinah refused to listen to Nooriya when she tried to tell her mother what she'd seen in the shop. By then, Sakinah was too far gone into her marriage, the gifts and endearments her husband showered her with, the carpet of rose petals on which she walked on her birthday. Her marriage was the talk of their community, women envied her for her house, piled high with every household product one could conceive of. If there was a new model of TV launched, her friends would flock to her house to test it out, confident that Farad would've already gifted it to her.

But then, what was not supposed to have happened took place. Thinking back, even now Sakinah wonders how her life would be today had she not picked up the phone that morning.

---

[20] How pretty is the girl, like a fairy.

That summer, one of Farad's cousins came to visit them from Bhendi Bazaar. And there was something about the way the two men laughed and whispered together that struck a suspicious chord.

'It was my birthday that day, you know. Farad had come back very late the night before and yet he'd woken early to make me breakfast in bed.'

He was downstairs when his phone had buzzed and Sakinah, with Nooriya's warnings fresh in her mind, had done something she'd never done before—picked it up and read his messages.

Her trembling fingers had found his cousin's message, asking Farad how Sakinah would react if she found out where they had been the night before. Farad had replied, 'Sakinah would never find out and even if she did, she'd cry for a while and then quieten down.'

'Soda water!' he'd added underneath.

We walk out, unable to sit in the room any longer. Outside, Sakinah has a tiny space enclosed by old rattan chicks. Its peaceful out here, like water held in the palm of the hand. The bamboo emanates a mild, pleasant fragrance reminding one of long-forgotten walks through a forest grove. The tiles under my feet are the pale green of Samarqand jade.

With Nooriya's encouragement, she had filed for divorce. The door of her home at Chai Chee had remained closed, so they had moved to Ben's house for a while. The Women's Charter[21] had ensured she receive what was rightfully hers. She had declined Farad's money and started working.

'But I wasn't satisfied, you know. I was greedy for more.'

Torn away from her family and friends, she had craved emotional acceptance. She would stay up entire nights wondering

---

[21] The Women's Charter of Singapore, 1961

if she had taken the right decision, if life would fall into place ever again, beat with its old, peaceful rhythm.

It was at this time that one night, on a momentary impulse, she wrote to the Syedna. She had poured out her life story, asking him if she'd taken the right decision, if she would ever find happiness again.

'I sent my *arzi*[22] to him and he wrote back with his blessings, even sent me *barakat*[23] with which to start my new life.'

His reply had changed her life. He hadn't encouraged her to file for divorce and yet had understood her decision. Finally, she'd found a love that didn't seek to change her, to advise her and mould her against her will; love that didn't expect her to suffer in silence. It simply accepted her the way she was with a quiet, sanctifying faith that set her free.

Sakinah had started wearing the ridah. She wanted to. She read the Holy Qur'an everyday so she could eventually become a *hafiz*.[24]

I look at Sakinah, the light from the setting sun is on her forehead. I no longer see any duality there. Her gentleness and vigour, her repose and restlessness have come together in a single-pointed calm, quivering determination to surrender.

'So, will Nooriya wear the ridah in Paris?' I ask before leaving.

'I don't know. It will be her decision,' she answers.

But I know, whatever it is, the decision will come from a place of strength.

I wave goodbye, looking back to see her where she stands, on the cooling jade, like water held in the palm of the hand.

---

[22] Plea, request
[23] Token money as sign of blessing.
[24] One who has memorized the whole Qur'an.

JUDAISM

Ecclesiastes 2:13

and I saw that wisdom has an advantage over folly,
as the advantage of light over darkness.

Judaism

What is remarkable about Judaism is the ripe and affirmative vision of human life and the divine that it upholds. Yahweh is 'apart' from creation and yet is considered 'a part' of creation. It's a faith lighted by a mystical insight that sees G_D[1] to be inhabiting every particle, thus sacralizing them. Consequently, Judaism does not deprecate the body, sexuality, or matter. Instead, it is a holistic, celebratory vision that believes that the soul is perfected by descending into this world.

Jews

The Jews are a widely mixed community—they could either be Ashkenazi Jews hailing from Eastern Europe, or Sephardic from around the Mediterranean. They could be settled in any part of the world and fit in anywhere on the sliding scale of their faith—from orthodox to reform congregations. In Singapore, too, there are the old settlers—an intimate group of a hundred individuals or less with some being even sixth-generation Singaporeans. Then there is the wider circle of the Israelis. With long-held diplomatic ties between the two countries, this is a well-consolidated group, coming to the island on different engagements and staying on average for anywhere between 3–5 years. And then there are the rest—an interesting medley from across the world, living in Singapore with varied professional or business interests. The overall number hovers around 3,000.

As in other aspects, in the case of the Jewish community, too, Singapore packs a punch well beyond its size. A community

---

[1] As believers of abstract monotheism, this is how Jews write the name of God. No one sees God, even Moses was granted only God's *kavod*, his holy essence or afterglow. He remains an abstract presence within everyone.

member notes the infrastructure that is available here, allowing Jews of every shade to practice their faith: there are four synagogues (two big ones in Waterloo Street and Oxley Rise, and two small ones at the Jacob Ballas Centre and the Jewish school), kosher restaurants and shop, Sir Manasseh Meyer International School, a home for the aged, a cemetery and funeral and burial services. Singapore is also home to the United Hebrew Congregation (UHC), Asia's largest non-orthodox Jewish congregation which believes in a synagogue without walls. While not forgetting Jewish rituals, they welcome mixed-faith couples or Jews with LGBTQ leanings. Despite the wide spectrum, community members—both orthodox and reformist—speak of the cohesiveness of the Jews of Singapore, with an annual community celebration that is often held in Sentosa. An interviewee who spent her youth rushing through the cities of the world—Hamburg, Lucerne, and Tehran—speaks of how it is in Singapore that she has found her final refuge. Among a people of the diaspora, her community feels at ease—the Jews, the first of the disenfranchised nations of perpetual immigrants.

Perhaps there are two important ways to understand how the Jewish community has been shaped and crafted over the years. The first is a religious one and goes back to the Jewish belief that humankind is not a slave or a victim but a co-creator with the divine, responsible for creation of divine life on earth. This implies, through worship and holy living, a seamless parallel can be forged between heaven and earth, and, as a corollary, it upgrades all overtures of a normal life. Thus, normal thoughts don't disturb divine thoughts; it rises up and sucks down divine thought and makes it a part of normal life, instead. Thus, the joy of the bride and the groom can be equivalent to the perfect joy created by God, the bridal canopy can be a parallel to Eden, and man and woman's creation of a child can be similar to God's creation of the universe. An interviewee while speaking of the purpose of Jewish life mentions, 'It's a faith of the pragmatic.' The focus firmly remains on a lifetime of upholding the *mitzvot*, commandments for leading the active life, where a baby can be welcomed with the blessing, *May he grow to a life of Torah, the wedding canopy and good deeds.* There is no hierarchy here and it is important to enjoy everyday encounters rather than expect a grand solution to life's riddles.

The second influencer is more of a cultural one. An important pointer in understanding the community is to accept that the Jews are a people of memory. They hold the memory of Israel close to their heart, the land of hills and valleys which, unlike Egypt, is not irrigated by the Nile but is meant to absorb the dew of heaven. The exile from Israel remains in collective memory and is perhaps the reason why the faith centres around minimum paraphernalia: everything of value is in their books and scrolls which travel with them. This is also the reason why Judaism has increasingly become less and less a faith to be believed in, but something that one does. The practice of Sabbath, for example, is a way to separate the kosher from the unclean, the sacred from profane, to define boundaries between themselves and others without depending on geographical walls. Hence also the Jewish dependence on symbolism: each synagogue with its eastern wall facing Jerusalem is a reminder of King Solomon's Temple, the challah bread of Sabbath reminiscent of the manna that fell from heaven, the *menorah* or nine-branched candelabrum of the number of days the lantern blazed in the Temple. They not only believe in their faith, but they live it, in the little everyday details and through the festivals, for otherwise, as the exiled people, they have no other way of reaffirming their deepest principles and values[2]. Thus, while one

---

[2] As an interesting way of navigating change and diverse cultural situations, Jews all over the world read the same section of the Torah on the same

interviewee speaks of the hundreds of little prayers that they device during the day—for eating, sleeping, and even for seeing the first flower of spring or a glorious sunset, another speaks of the 'Let's eat the book festival' or the Rosh Hashanah when they eat food with Aramaic names that evoke biblical passages, like honey, dates, pomegranates, etc.

As the divine and the everyday, the tactile and the transcendental intertwine in inextricable ways, it is left to the woman to play the all-important role of an intermediary. It is she who, for the last one hundred years after the candle-lighting and blessing and the uttering of the *Yehi Ratzon* (May it be thy will), has added another prayer for the restoration of the temple, for in its redemption lies the final sanctification of Jewish life. Interviewees disagree vehemently when told that the Jewish women enjoy the private rather than the public experience of their faith, that they light the prayer candle at home rather than read the Torah at the synagogue. Instead, they say, their physical looks and duties move on a sliding scale depending on whether they are part of reformist or orthodox congregations. It's also determined by individual choice—some cover their hair under a wig or scarf and wear clothes till below the knee, while others do not.

A member of the community refers to an important word in Judaism—*binah*. It roughly translates into the power to understand, to make sophisticated connections, and penetrate to the deeper meanings of life. Some equate it to common sense, and according to believers, binah comes more naturally to women than to men. In explaining this, the interviewee speaks of crossing the threshold of forty and

---

day. The cycle of reading the Torah begins on the Sabbath following the festival of Simchat Torah in autumn, and ends with the Simchat Torah of the following year.

attaining middle-age. It is at this time, when youth with its quixotic expectations of justice and recompense is over, and past realities have collapsed, that we, for the first time, challenge the self-definitions that have sustained us so far. 'It is a tricky time,' she says, 'when we look at ourselves in the mirror and say, "This is it!" In Jewish life, this is a time when one learns Hebrew and masters Torah-reading more seriously than ever before, so that meaning returns to life. But it is the woman,' she adds, 'more naturally inclined towards nurture, generativity, and interdependence, who moves with better ease into middle-aged life and the understanding that life is imperfect.' That every life is incomplete, that even Moses died without completing his last project of redeeming his people from slavery.

Irrespective of where they stand on the spectrum between orthodox and reformist, certain duties, however, are sacrosanct only to the Jewish woman—the lighting of the Sabbath candles, taking the challah[3] out of the Sabbath dough, and dipping in the *mikvah*[4] waters in preparation to creating new life. What is interesting is the theme that unifies the three actions—it is the feminine ability to kindle and nurture the spark of holiness in every particle of earth. As the *Song of Songs* mentions, he sought God everywhere and finally placed him in a mother's womb, the seed from which God is born.

---

[3] This is according to the *mitzvah* or commandment that requires a small olive-sized part of the dough to be set aside before the baking of the Sabbath bread commences. This is to abide by the divine verdict that when the Jewish people entered Israel, anyone who baked bread was to give a portion of their bread to the priests who worked at the temple.

[4] A pool of water, some of which is from a fresh source, where a Jewish woman takes a dip every month after her menstrual cycle. It needs to be mentioned that men dip here, too, often as part of their spiritual preparation.

The whole of creation waits with trembling anticipation for the messiah.

* * *

Mahalla (Neighbourhood)

Among all the Jewish women I met, it is TT or Tikvah Teherani (name changed) who remains my mita or 'friend of memories'. As we met sometimes at a café by the conduit of commerce called Clemenceau Avenue or at a club, I saw in her the many selves that make up her 'self'. After a lifetime of travel, she was quite accustomed to the long wait at every new stopover, as the soul reassembled itself, bit by bit, scattered without knowing at a lakeside or a façade of bas-relief. Singapore was her refuge, where she felt no need to retract her soul, drag it back to attach to her body. She could loiter awhile instead, thinking through her multiplicity among a community of fellow-travellers.

It was amazing how many times she had tried to build bridges—a class reunion with a group of girls she studied with in Switzerland, a meet up with an uncle who had long left Hamburg and settled in LA—each time only to find she has changed beyond recognition and could not fit herself back in the mould she had cast for herself—the angel in the snow was a cold still-life.

It was difficult to watch her anguish as she made a rapid pendulum swing towards childhood, in a mad scramble for that one memory that would set her free; for she remains, like murraya entwined to a fence after the rails have been uprooted, a part of two worlds. I watched as she bent over double picking up the pieces and, in her shadows, Naomi emerged, both tied together by violent memories, bloodstains in the snow.

TT pointed in the general direction of Waterloo Street and told Naomi, 'You go down Sophia Hill, cross Bencoolen Street, and there you have it, the oldest synagogue of Singapore, with a *mikvah* of fresh water and the nicest *mikvah* lady[5] you can come across, she will treat you like a princess!'

It was her usual sales pitch, though she doubted this couple would fall for it. The real-estate market was a difficult place to be in nowadays, business from the embassy was running dry. She fervently hoped this deal with Mr and Mrs Edelman would work out, otherwise she worried about her shrinking monthly commission.

As it is, she was not in the best of moods today, what with the message she had received in the morning. Aviva, as usual curt to the point of being rude . . . TT's anxious fingers searched for her phone in her pocket. *Uncle Abraham dead, found today morning, rather last evening, LA time.*

When? How? TT still couldn't believe it. She'd spoken to him only last week. How would she ever manage to survive without him? In fact, it was Uncle Abraham who had given her this name—TT. Her parents had called her Tikvah Teherani, 'hope' in Persian. But when she was bullied in school, it was he who suggested they change it. And she'd realized that TT was a name she could live with. It was quick and snazzy, and, above all, had a bit of Uncle Abraham in it.

'So, you're from Israel?' she forced herself to focus on Naomi. Looked at her intently—the blue wig from under which dark strands had escaped, the rather unfeminine, high, flat-bridged nose, the full lips plumped up in nude pink, like a statement across her face.

---

[5] The lady who in complete privacy guides a Jewish woman through the monthly purification ritual.

'Nope,' Naomi had cut her off, sharp as a whip.

TT hesitated for a moment. She could have sworn the message from the embassy said they were travelling from Tel Aviv. Was she wrong?

She shifted her gaze to Naomi's husband. Naomi's eyes somehow intimidated her, with their adamant will to look beyond TT. There was a wall in there.

Just behind Naomi stood her husband, with his mop of curls, a pinched, waxy look, a checked shirt that carried every wrinkle and curve of his body. TT extended her hand to him.

'Welcome to Singapore, Mr Edelman,' she said.

'Hi–I–am–Nathan–but–you–can–call–me–Nat!' The reply came in the breathless rush of either a shy man or someone who thought such mundane matters did not warrant his time.

TT sighed; it was clearly not going to be easy.

She ushered the couple inside the apartment, walked them to the bay windows at the end of the drawing room. Sophia Hill stretched before them, drenched in sunlight. It was the time of morning when officegoers had left for work and children had been bundled off in school buses. From the twelfth-floor window, all they could see were leafy tops of trees, hear cuckoo calls floating up. It was the burbling silence of a flowing river— luminous and eloquent.

There used to be a similar kind of peace at their home, too, on Sabbath[6] evenings. The evenings which are now many years in the past, at their home in Hamburg, where Maamaan always laid a place for Uncle Abraham at their Sabbath table.

---

[6] A day stretching from Friday evening to Saturday evening when a Jewish family abstains from work, and which is dedicated to religious observance.

Uncle Abraham, with whom Friday evenings would be so much fun. It was he who had taught her to play the game they called Sound of Silence.

He would sit on the largest wingchair in their living room because that was the only chair that could hold his girth, pull a camelhair blanket across his legs, giving her a bit of it to tuck around her feet as she sat perched on the arm of his chair. TT would watch as his chest rose and fell, after a while the shirt-button tightly stretched across his stomach, popping open. Taking turns, they would close their eyes and guess the sound that came from any part of the house. In the candlelit silence they could hear the smallest of sounds—Baabaa flipping a page of the letter that had come from his family in Iran, the click-click of Daniel or David moving the Scrabble tiles, the little sizzle as the Shabbos candles[7] burnt down to their tallow.

Finally, there would only be quiet. TT would sit with her eyes closed, her cheeks flushed with the wine and the heat from the blanket. She would hear Uncle Abraham breathe, and beyond that, the world outside their house—the crackle as ice contracted on the frozen Lake Alster, the swish of a night-bird as it made its way to the moon.

'. . . it was Brooklyn all the way, in Seagate—the only beach town in Flatbush.'

TT turned around to Naomi, catching only the tail-end of what she'd said. Both of them stood at the window, their elbows on the grainy, white-washed window sill. TT felt herself flush, it was not often that she missed what her client was saying.

'Beg your pardon?' she asked.

---

[7] Sabbath candles lit on Friday evening before sunset to welcome Jewish Sabbath.

Naomi looked at her as if noticing her for the first time. Her quick eyes took in TT's embarrassment.

'I was saying that Israel was just a stopover for a week while we were travelling to Singapore. Otherwise, we are Brookliners all the way, for the last ten years,' she repeated in a kindlier tone.

TT thought it was time that she gave her sales pitch another push. She pointed in the direction of Waterloo Street again, offered helpfully, 'This is the old Jewish mahalla of Singapore, Mrs Edelman. You'll find nothing much has changed.'

But in response, she noticed Naomi's face stiffen. 'I too grew up in a . . . mahalla, as you call it,' she remarked, in a voice that sounded as terse as it had done before.

TT cringed a bit at her tone. Was that something wrong she had said? She thought it was a nice, familiar touch . . .

'In B'nai Brak. Yes, Shacked up right in the orthodox heartland.' Naomi paused, her mind obviously going over some unhappy memory. 'Phew! It's crazy, that place . . . on a Sabbath afternoon, not even a child cries for candy!'

'My wife, of course, shook it up,' Nat rushed in, casting an affectionate look at Naomi, 'Mimi with her *menorah*[8] leggings and the tetragrammaton on her nails!'

TT's eyes fell on Naomi's fingernails. Her sluggish mind unwillingly noted the name of Yahweh painted in manicured perfection on her four fingers—YHWH.[9]

But Naomi was already turning away, disdainfully tossing over her shoulder, 'Well, that place really needed shaking up.

---

[8] The golden lamp of seven branches in the Temple of Jerusalem.

[9] The Hebrew name of God transliterated in four letters as *YHWH* or *JHVH* and articulated as *Yahweh* or *Jehovah*.

It was as dead as the stupid bottling plant where you worked,'
leaving Nat to cover her tracks with an embarrassed guffaw.

They had stayed in the Jewish quarters of Hamburg, too—TT's
family: Maamaan, Baabaa, her sister Aviva, her brothers Daniel
and David, and Uncle Abraham, of course. They had stayed
in Grindel with its square with a weird void in the middle,
where the old synagogue had been bombed off. Yes, the Jewish
mahalla, but it didn't really help.

No, living in Grindel did not eventually save Uncle Abraham.
He and Baabaa used to deal in Persian carpets then—hand-
knotted ones, each with its own unique design of pomegranates
and cypress trees, and brave Shahs going off on a hunt of leopards,
sourced from places with musical names—Esfahan, Qum,
Tabriz. Their warehouse was near the port. But one night, Uncle
Abraham's warehouse burnt down completely to its stumps. And
with it went his entire stock of carpets, carpets which he had
bought with the money from selling his house in Teheran.

TT remembered that night. Maamaan had forgotten to draw
the curtains and Lake Alster stretched outside their window in
an expanse of frigid silver. Against it was the silhouette of Uncle
Abraham, leaning forward with his elbows on the table, shoulders
slumped, his face cupped in the palm of his hands. Her parents
tried to convince him it was one of those freak accidents of winter,
a carelessly doused fire licking at the log-pile of the warehouse. But
Uncle Abraham merely shook his head, refusing to look up. 'No,
no, no, it's me . . . it's me again,' he muttered, 'it's time to move,
move before I put everyone else in danger.'

'I remember we would move continuously in my
childhood,' Naomi was saying. She had come to stand next to
TT where she lingered aimlessly in the middle of the drawing
room, where the sun fell in an elongated finger across the floor,
like a rolled-out yoga mat.

'My grandparents were holocaust survivors in Poland. I grew up with them. And though the war was long over and the dust had settled, we were never really left alone. And so we moved,' Naomi sighed, 'Again, and then again. First to Madrid and then to Lisbon—each time staying in a Jewish neighbourhood. Till in B'nai Brak, I decided I'd had enough—the same cycle of walking to the synagogue and the *zemirot*[10] singing and the gatherings around the Sabbath table—I needed to turn around and snip off the shadow.'

And so, she'd washed up ashore at Flatbush, started her boutique, a little hole-in-the-wall where she sold hair scrunchies and leggings and painted nails—all in Jewish design.

In the distance, they could hear Nat. He was walking from room to room checking the aircons, the sound of the remote striking a pleasant tremolo. As he moved, he jauntily whistled *Da Dayenu*.[11] The two women smiled at each other; it was a tune they both knew well.

TT followed Naomi as she left the living room. She was a bit hesitant now to show her the other Jewish features of the house—the mantelpiece for placing the Shabbos candles, the little tables for the prayer books, the painting of an old Judenstern lamp[12] from Germany which had been such a draw for her previous clients.

She showed her instead the freshly renovated washroom with double vanity, the walk-in closet with concealed lighting; watched Naomi run her fingertips down the wardrobe shelves, her tightly-clenched jawline seeming to relax a little.

---

[10] Jewish hymns, normally sung in Hebrew or Aramaic, sometimes in Yiddish or Ladino, too.

[11] *Dayenu* is an ancient seder hymn sung during Pesach or Passover, approximately translating to 'It would have been enough . . .'

[12] The hanging Sabbath lamp, usually made of brass.

'This is nice,' Naomi said, twirling round in front of the floor-length mirror, her full-bodied skirt flouncing around her like a little girl's dress.

The overhead light shone on the golden menorah Naomi wore as a brooch. Her face was close to the mirror now, she was cleaning lipstick from her teeth with a fierce intensity.

'This is exactly the way I like it,' she said through a mouth held open in an 'O', 'alone, with no shadows behind.'

Uncle Abraham was all alone, too. He seemed quite happy to think of them as his family, though. Yet, after that winter when his warehouse burnt down, he had insisted he'd move to LA. He had a nephew who stayed there, the only remaining member of his extended family.

On some Sabbath evenings, when Baabaa read his letters from his family in Iran, Uncle Abraham would pull out a photograph from his chest pocket. He would stare at it for long minutes, and TT would know he wanted to talk about her.

'Her' was a young woman in pigtails, smiling into the sun, wearing an apron, with a keg of potato at her feet. 'Her' was she who had written behind the photograph in a cheeky, slanted hand the lines by Hafez, 'Look not upon the dimple of her chin, danger lurks there!'

Abigail, the only woman Uncle Abraham ever loved. The two had met when they were students at the Hebrew University of Jerusalem. They worked as volunteers at a *kibbutz*,[13] a communal farm. A rich businessman's daughter, Abigail did not know any housework and would take fifteen minutes to peel one potato. 'And you know the shirts she burned, hundreds of them, burned through with a hole in their chest!' Uncle Abraham would say and laugh till tears rolled from his eyes.

---

[13] A collective community unique to Israel.

TT would join in, but she knew what was coming next. Uncle Abraham and Abigail used to help pick out weeds in the war trenches at the kibbutz, not knowing that the trenches would come in use so soon. But then lo and behold, the Six-Day War had rolled along and Abigail had stepped on a land-mine unknowingly.

'And it was all gone, all of her, blown to smithereens, shirt and potato and smile and all.'

The photograph of Abigail was all he had of her.

TT's reverie was broken by a squeal, almost like an excited child's. She spun around. Unknown to her, Naomi had moved away, walked towards the kitchen.

Naomi and Nat stood with their back to her. Naomi's vivid blue hair was swept to one side, and from where she stood at the kitchen door, TT could see the Star of David[14] that was tattooed on her nape. Nat rubbed it with the tip of his thumb, almost as if it was a talisman for staying connected. From behind, they looked travel-stained, tired.

Naomi turned around, 'This is so . . . so kosher!' she said. 'The heating plate, the double sink[15] . . . it's something like what Gran used to have.' Her voice trailed off, sounding bemused.

TT sighed, there went her hope of clinching the deal of the month! She'd known all along that something like this was going to happen.

'Well, I can make a special request to the landlord to renovate,' she offered by way of explanation. But Naomi had

---

[14] Unique sign of Jewish identity.

[15] Parts of a kosher kitchen. The heating plate is a tin or copper sheet usually made by the tinsmith in a Jewish neighbourhood. It covers a burner or several burners and is used to keep food warm during Sabbath since all the cooking is done before Sabbath commences. A double sink is used to separate meat and dairy.

already turned away, poking her head into cupboards, reaching up to the larder to see if the hinges worked.

TT walked back to the living room, stood by the window. The house was chilly with all the aircons turned on. She felt shivery, the cold gave her goosebumps.

Who would be joining Uncle Abraham's *Shiva*[16] at LA, she wondered? The nephew had never taken care of Uncle Abraham. He had lived alone in a small apartment that looked on to the grey cemented walls of the state electricity board. Who would remember to cover him with his *tallith*[17]? Remember to snip off a fringe and make it defective? And for that matter, now with Uncle Abraham gone, who would TT speak to every Sunday? Speak about Maamaan and Baabaa and their house in Hamburg, the house by the Lake Alster?

Not all Friday evenings in Hamburg were equally peaceful, though. There were certain days when Baabaa and Uncle Abraham would come back from *shul*,[18] bristling with a sense of purpose, and TT would watch Uncle Abraham finger the spice box,[19] the little pewter box darting to and fro between his fingers, seeming to dance with the tension.

---

[16] A Hebrew word meaning 'seven', refers to a seven-day period of formalized mourning by the immediate family of the deceased, beginning immediately after burial.

[17] A prayer shawl with God's blessing embroidered on it, it has fringes on four corners called the *tzizith*, the name of Yahweh is in the knots of the tassels. One of the sets of fringes is snipped at the time of burial as a sign of release.

[18] Synagogue

[19] The spice box, usually made of pewter or silver, contains clove and myrtle leaves and is used in the closing ceremony of Sabbath. The perfume ritual is conducted over the spice box. According to Kabbalistic communities, man receives an extra soul on the evening before Sabbath. The soul releases its pungency and returns to the world of souls at the end of the Sabbath.

And then, crashing through the complete silence, the phone would ring.

The walls of their house would echo with the sound and TT would hear the flutter of wings as nesting birds flew into the night.

On normal Sabbath days, they would not have answered the phone.[20] But today was special. It was her grandfather, her *pedar-e bozorg*[21] calling from Teheran. Uncle Abraham would pounce on the phone while Baabaa and Maamaan craned to hear.

It would be a long conversation about a house-boy, a *farrash,* and a *morgh*, a chicken. Had he bought the chicken from the bazaar, had he cleaned it properly, had he plucked its feathers till nothing remained?

TT would almost fall asleep, wondering why *pedar-e bozorg* was having so many parties nowadays? Why was their *maader-e bozorg*[22] not able to ever have her chickens properly cleaned?

It was only years later that Uncle Abraham told her that chicken was a code word for passport, they were helping families escape to Germany even as Iran went up in flames.

And, in a couple of weeks, their Sabbath dinner would get even bigger. Maamaan would light an extra candle for the family that was joining them and the children would watch as the adults broke out in excited Farsi. Once Aviva, always a bit blunt, had asked, 'Is Maamaan the only one who can clean chicken properly, so you have to come all the way to Hamburg to eat?' Everyone around the table had burst out laughing.

---

[20] A phone call can be taken during Sabbath only if it is a matter of life or death.

[21] Farsi word for grandfather.

[22] Farsi word for grandmother.

TT smiled at the memory, not hearing Naomi come up behind her. She did not hear till Naomi placed her hand on her shoulder and TT felt the warmth of her hand seep in through her blouse.

'We'll take the house,' TT heard her say.

She slowly turned around. Naomi stood just behind her. The light from the window picked out her smudged eyeliner, the streaks of black on her cheeks.

'I never went back, you know? Never. Not even when Gran was dying . . . I couldn't bear to.'

The tremor in Naomi's voice was evident.

On Sabbath evenings, Maamaan's hair would always smell nice. She'd light the candles and whisper her prayers, and then turn around to place her hand in blessing on TT's head, kiss her on her forehead.[23] That kiss was precious. Aviva and TT would race to stand next to Maaman. Even now, TT could smell the lavender in Maamaan's freshly washed hair and feel the warmth of her lips.

TT reached out to hold Naomi's hand.

'But we never left,' she said in a low voice, 'none of us did.'

The morning outside had folded in. Like the petals of a flower, it held Sophia Hill in its golden embrace.

---

[23] The woman encircles the light three times with her hands and repeats 'Blessed be He and blessed be His name' with each circling, and then turns around to bless the person standing next to her. What is often overlooked is that a Jewish festival, be it Sabbath or Passover, is mostly a joyous celebration. Maybe it is during such festivals that the truth of the words 'Go, eat your bread in gladness and drink your wine in joy, for your action was long ago approved by God' (Ecclesiastes, 9:7–9) is most evident.

HINDUISM

Bhagavad Gita, 13:17

he is the light of all lights which shines beyond all darkness,
it is vision, the end of vision, to be reached by vision,
dwelling in the heart of all.

Hinduism

At the centre of Hindu belief is the ultimate reality that is forever nameless, formless, and beyond definition, the 'Brahman'. The Sanskrit word has a dual etymology—*br* i.e., 'to breathe' and *brih* i.e., 'to be great', and in extension, it is tempting to believe that if one breathes, one has the chance to be 'great'. The Brahman or Absolute Reality is conceived to be the presence of Pure Being, Pure Consciousness and Pure Bliss. It is this indivisible and eternal unity that lies underneath the confusing multiplicity of Hinduism, the vast pantheon of gods, with often overlapping attributes. The ideal Hindu life is one that is calm, fearless, and selfless, residing in the knowledge that each individual soul is one with the everlasting Brahman.

Nattukottai Chettiars

Numbering at around 1,000 families, the Nattukottai Chettiars is another mercantile community of Singapore, though with a significant difference. While traditionally given to money lending and banking businesses, for the last half-a-century or so, the compass has shifted and they have emerged mostly as working-class professionals. As a community member smilingly remarks, 'The change is so complete that a father will not give his daughter in marriage to a moneylender now, only to a professional!'

Interestingly, though a part of the predominant Tamil community of Singapore, the Chettiars do maintain their distinct identity on most accounts. Old-fashioned Chettiar homes, for instance, use the Tamil tongue of Chettinad and Madurai while, otherwise, the Tamil of Thanjavur district is spoken in Singapore. Thus, the word 'mother', central to most Asian cultures, is *Amma* in Tamil but becomes *Aathaa* in Chettiar homes, and so the difference of dialects continues. Such differentiating gaps, however, are dwindling. A younger member of the community mentions how she feels closer to the mainstream Tamil culture of Singapore than the traditions of Chettinad, adhered to today mostly by expats.

Chettinad in south Tamil Nadu was the land of the Nattukottai Chettiars, specifically the seventy-five villages that dot the 600 square mile area between Pudukkottai in the north and Sivaganga in the south. Among these, Kadaikudi is the largest village, a veritable antique lovers' paradise with its palatial houses that gleam with teak from Burma, satinwood from Ceylon and marble from Italy. Add to this the diamonds from Golconda and pearls from the Gulf of Mannar with which the exquisite jewellery of the Chettiar women were crafted, and one would understand the reason for the life-size safes that adorn the traditional Chettiar home!

But these majestic houses also point to another direction— the rich yields that the Nattukottai Chettiars carried with them to whichever part of the world they travelled to on business. In Singapore, they were known to be one of the richest communities. Like the famous Alkaff or Alsagoff[1] families, they brought money to invest in Singapore, rather than creating capital in this little island.

Well, what created such wealth that folklores are made of? It was the Nattukottai Chettiars' willingness to travel. They were among the first from India to brave the *kaalapani*[2] or the churning oceans. Under the Chola dynasty, they sailed

---

[1] Arab families of Singapore.
[2] The black water of the seven seas; once crossed, it demanded a purifying ritual.

as far as Malacca and Sumatra and met in the islands of the East. Such carefully nurtured trade connections with the East augured well, and under the colonial masters, their businesses swelled. In Singapore, the first Nattukottai Chettiars arrived in the 1820s, and soon, their *kittangis* or financial cooperatives, each easily employing thirty to forty people, lined the business district around the Singapore River. In these shophouses, where the Chettiars lived and worked, brisk business was conducted in Bazaar Malay, the hand-written accounts always impeccable and above reproach. 'It was a whole super-structure out there, a whole system put carefully in place so business would succeed,' says an interviewee whose family ran a kittangi for three consecutive generations, while speaking of the intricate networks of familial and village bonds on which Chettiar business was built.

Yet, the idyll was short-lived. First, it was the tumult of the Great Depression and then the tightening moneylending laws. If, across the region, it was a rising tide of nationalism that singled out this small community—which by the 1950s owned a predominant share of the economy—in independent Singapore, it was the government's focus on regulating the banking industry. As kittangis wound up, the changed circumstances triggered a need to reinvent themselves. What followed was a period of dire struggle during which the values that had accompanied their hard-nosed business acumen—filial piety, religiosity, frugality and a conscientious industriousness—stood them in good stead.

Belief runs deep that it was the conservative roots that helped the community survive, even resurrect itself. Indulgent of no wealth-depleting habits like drinking or smoking, an interviewee speaks of an 'almost miserly sense of propriety' among the Chettiars, while another elderly member speaks of the temple which has always been the fountainhead of Chettiar social life. 'Entertainment last time not much, nowadays have.

Before only Chettiar temple entertainment—singing, dancing, Thaipusam, Navaratri, everything in temple,' the old *achi*[3] says with an endearing sweetness.

Now, what does the life of a woman entail in this community of merchants-turned-professionals, self-confessedly not 'cool' as they follow their traditional ways?

A story that dominates popular imagination is of a Chola king who had lusted after and abducted a Chettiar girl. A community that prides itself in the chastity of its women, the Chettiars hadn't hesitated to revolt, though it was in the safe sanctuary of the Chola kingdom that they played a leading business role. The tradition continued and the elderly *achi* speaks of how, as a young girl back in India, she managed her father's estate while the men of the house were away on business for as long as three years at a stretch. 'I managed the house, the tank, the temple, I rotated money even,' she says, and yet all was skillfully managed while she stayed indoors and delegated the work to trusty family retainers.

In Singapore, the Chettiar women started arriving only in the 1950s, by when the winds of change were already gathering. Though peppered by numerous women working professionals today, women's life in orthodox households has been marked by a fine balancing act. If in the past they had to manage their vast households while maintaining feminine modesty, today they have cast themselves in the role of a modern woman, and yet cannot ignore the calls to convention from their temple and community.

And beyond that? Beyond that is the legendary Chettiar hospitality and the delicious cuisine of Chettinad—the *pachadi*, the *poriyal*—some available in restaurants, some only as home-

---

[3] Aunt

grown recipes. There is also the Tamil Tirumurai, popular among the Chettiars of Singapore—a compendium of songs and an important literary yield of the Bhakti tradition of worship that swept across India from the eighth century onwards and made Vedic traditions accessible to the masses.

But even beyond that, and maybe wider in its impact, is the celebration of Singapore's beloved Thaipusam festival. Celebrated at the Tank Road temple[4] of the Nattukottai Chettiars, the festival attracts members of other communities, and, over the years, has grown from a ten-day affair to being stretched over a month.

While speaking about the temple in Tank Road temple where worship is offered to Murugan or Kartikeya,[5] achi narrates an incident that occurred in her past. Her young son had been caught in a terrible road accident, and she had gone to sleep crying that night. In her sleep, she had dreamed of Murugan. He had touched her son's leg thrice with his *vel*[6], and the next day, achi had returned to SGH[7], secure in her knowledge that her son would be better. Sure enough, skin grafting had been done to his leg over three surgeries, and he had been able to resume normal life. 'Our faith is nothing but trust,' she concludes with a sweet sense of complacency.

---

[4] The more-than-a-century old Sri Thendayuthapani Temple of Singapore. Here, while in the main sanctum there is the much-decorated idol of Lord Murugan as the prince and son of Lord Shiva and Goddess Parvati, at the back, in an alcove in the wall, is the figure of Lord Kartikeya where he stands as a young boy stripped down to his loin cloth, seeking nothing but spiritual wisdom. This idol is fashioned after the idol in the renowned Indian temple of Palani.

[5] Murugan or Kartikeya are the names of the same God, other commonly used names are Skanda, Kumara, Mahasena, Shanmukha, and Subrahmanya. He is the Hindu God of War.

[6] Spear or lance

[7] Singapore General Hospital

If one visits the temple, one can see Hindu tradition at its best. If there is an endearing intimacy in the rituals of dressing and feeding the child Kartikeya, as Lord Murugan, he offers the grand orchestration of spiritual profundity. Here he is the prince— proud and victorious, but also a young wayfarer on his final quest, who, after travelling across *Triloka*,[8] stands stripped to his loin cloth, seeking nothing but the knowledge of realms beyond. Here, one sees devotees traverse daily the path between the ritualistic and the philosophical, the manifest and the unmanifested, a path the navigation to which is enabled only by love.

* * *

Brahman

The day I first met her, my mita or 'friend of love', rain kept me boring company. As I walked down the corridors of NUS, the ones where students work on last-minute submissions with such fierce concentration that one feels compelled to creep by, I noticed her feet had left water marks down the hallway. They were like the footsteps of the goddess of prosperity we draw on our threshold to welcome her home. Only this goddess wore sports shoes.

I don't remember if at this point there actually was a streak of lightning that illuminated the flowers of a flame tree, or it was my flight of fancy. But I did see her in all her beauty—a complexion that reflected the overcast sky layered with clouds, her voice that held the low rumble of thunder, of passions she'd felt but never expressed. Vistas opened up behind the NUS walls—the golden spire of a village temple where generations of her forefathers had worshipped, the high, treacherous wind that rushes through the choultry,[9] ruffling

---

[8] The three realms of Hindu belief.
[9] Resting place for pilgrims.

the hyacinth in the tank. And as she spoke, the smaller moments of her life entered my imagination, became my own.

Later I met her at the Tank Road Temple, the only woman clad in jeans, glancing anxiously at her watch among all the jasmine-scented women, and I saw in her the compulsions of a great love. It rose without her knowing, like vapours that rise from a seething caldera. For isn't it the Tirukkuṟaḷ[10] that mentions 'They say love is the reason why this soul of ours is bound with bone'?

They stumbled out of the MRT station. Vishnupriya, the Chinese construction worker with a phoenix tattooed on his nape, the woman with hair that smelt of matcha—all of them. They travelled together almost every evening, all the way from Jurong East to Tanah Merah, squished together like lovers in a darkened theatre. Every evening their knuckles on the straphangers whitened with two needs—the urge to get home and the urge to ignore each other. While Vishnupriya spent much of the long ride staring at the powerful talons of the phoenix and listening to Murugan songs on her earphones, the woman played Candy Crush. The bird fascinated Vishnupriya, bringing to mind thoughts of the young, brave Murugan tearing the body of the demon into two. And as her body swayed to the gentle rhythm of the train, her eyes gradually glazed over, the two images merging into one.

Yet today was different. Even as the old, squeaky escalator brought her into the light of early evening, she was quickly engulfed in the commotion. It was not the routine evening

---

[10] By Tamil poet Thiruvalluvar, the Tirukkuṟaḷ is a classic Sangam text speaking about virtue, wealth and love. Despite its didactic purpose, aficionados appreciate it for its sheer poetry.

chaos—taxis turning from green to a preoccupied red; hungry officegoers impatiently watching the ticker box for their bus. Today it was something more compelling—there had been a storm in the afternoon and one of the asbestos sheets that pulled a veil of modesty over the excavation work on the new MRT line had fallen in.

She joined the gathering crowd and watched in awe. It was as if a whole new vista had opened up underground, inviting, yet intimidating. The grounds, the canyons, the mountains of rubble were spread on a much larger scale than her city was accustomed to. Construction workers in their yellow rubber boots were miniatures against the contours of the gorges that cut in deep. She saw the layers of fiery red laterite soil covered in a squelchy mucilage shimmer in the evening light. It took her step by step into the very belly of the earth, till she heard nothing but the echoing, hollow sound of heavy bulldozers, smelled the raw, primeval smell of parts unexplored for many years.

The sight unsettled her. Vishnupriya looked around. Her co-passengers had already moved on. The Chinese man was lighting a much-awaited cigarette by the bin. The woman was already rounding the corner, Vishnupriya could see the surprisingly clean undersoles of her stilettoes.

She knew she needed to hurry back too. It was the second-last day of Skanda Sasti[11], the penultimate day of celebrations

---

[11] While according to the Hindu calendar Sasti is observed every lunar fortnight (i.e., the sixth day of the waxing moon and the sixth day of the waning moon), Skanda Sasti marks the big annual celebration of Lord Murugan defeating the two demons, Soorapadman and Tarakasura, denoting the end of evil and restoration of peace. Skanda Sasti celebrations occur in the month of *Aipassi* (mid Oct–mid Nov), and at the Tank Road Temple, it takes place over six days when devotees fast during the day (the fasting normally commences on the day after Deepavali), and every evening

at the temple. Her family would be waiting for her at home—Agasthya, Aathaa, her son Shravanan—once she arrived, they would all get ready and leave for the Murugan temple.

Yet there was something about the evening that made her hang back, stand with her elbows on the rails, and watch the pandemonium that the asbestos sheet had revealed, the colossal horizon of heaving, sweltering mass. Surprisingly, it was nice to feel the steamy air that rose moiled with speckles of the bloodied ground. Here, she felt alive, part of a living, breathing thing.

She knew the sight that awaited her at home. The darkened living room with curtains drawn, Agasthya and his mother on the sofa. As she entered, she'd need to deaden her senses, dull them to an anesthetized indifference till she felt nothing at all: didn't hear the sound of the TV, the high-pitched, feverish fury in the Indian anchor's voice as he provided live coverage of the Skanda Sasti celebrations at the Tiruchendur Temple[12] of Tamil Nadu, did not hear the contempt in Agasthya's voice as he looked up and said, 'I've been calling your son to come and watch the programme, but he doesn't want to. He is becoming a complete Singaporean, that boy!'

---

there is a coordinated chanting of the Tamil *Archanai* by several hundreds, over several cycles, so that at the end of the six days, the God's name is chanted at least 100,000 times. The evening celebrations at the Tank Road Temple end on the penultimate day. On the last day, the chanting is done in the morning, followed by *Abishegam* (pouring of the holy water to the *vel* in the main altar), *Alankaram* (decoration of the idol), and *Puja*. Here, unlike the other temples of SG, the pulling of Kartikeya's silver chariot around the temple grounds, and his final symbolical slashing of the demons are not the highlights of the celebrations due to reasons of legacy.

[12] This temple is the second of the six Arupadai Veedu temples or the six abodes of Kartikeya temples in India (the six abodes are Thiruparankundram, Tiruchendur, Palani, Swamimalai, Thiruthani, and Pazhamudircholai), and hence the celebrations of Skanda Sasti occur on a very large scale here.

'But he is, he is a Singaporean!' Vishnupriya would protest despite herself. Her voice would be swallowed by the loud incantation of the television and Agasthya would have already turned away, sliding lower on the sofa, his eyes glittering with the seething images of gathering devotees.

And like every day, she would have to push her annoyance aside, struggle to control her temper as she went to her room, tore through her sarees finding the right one—a *kanjivaram* silk the colour of a peacock's neck. For Agasthya liked her to dress well when they went to the temple, for it would never do to let the old achis gossip and conjecture if Agasthya was making enough money on his job to keep his family well provided.

She would hurriedly drape the saree around her and rush to Shravanan's room to get him ready and find his room in a . . . Or would she find him at all today? After what had happened that morning, would he be there, sitting slouched on his beanbag, images from his phone flickering in his spectacles, waiting for her to come home, as he did every day—her son, born after two whole years of prayers offered to Murugan, with a complexion that shimmered like blue luminescence in the moonlight?

Panic hastened her footsteps. Vishnupriya panted a little as she turned into the road, leading off the main street that would take her to her condo. This stretch was a bit uphill, she would have to reach the crest before she could see the setting sun below the horizon, like a looming fireball. Under her breath, she muttered lines from the Skanda Sasti Kavacam, *O son of Shiva, dweller of the heart, come daily to protect me.* Amma used to say that the words protected Murugan's devotees like an armour. It was Appa who had taught them to her; Appa, on their first visit back to their village.

Vishnupriya was six when they first went back to Kundrakudi[13]. She was young but not too young to realize how her father seemed like a new man the moment they crossed the borders, into their village. Appa, in his clean white veshti,[14] with a stringy moustache drooping over his lip that he combed with a quick flick of his pocket comb.

Appa, the mild-mannered man who never could make a success of his palm-oil business and whose example Amma cited while invoking the worst scourges of her life. Appa, who had stood that day in chest-deep water in the tank of their village in Kundrakudi, moving aside the water-hyacinth with his arms, stumbling a bit as the long waterweeds caught at his ankles, calling out to her, 'Priya, Priya en chellam.[15] Come into the water. See? It is not cold.'

But six-year-old, city-bred Vishnupriya had been scared: scared of the water, scared of the pilasters of vividly coloured yali[16] faces that surrounded them in the temple, scared of sleeping that night in the open yard of the choultry, under a dark sky.

She had slept as close to Appa as she possibly could, with her face against his back, hearing his rattling asthmatic breath rise and fall like a shuttle in a loom. She had woken early to the sound of silence, the swish of bat wings in the air, a distant rustle of palmyra leaves. And then, even as she pressed her head to her pillow, she heard, as if emerging from the hidden light of the pigeon-neck sky, the first golden notes of the morning raga.

Appa stood at the door of the temple playing his flute.

---

[13] A village in the Sivaganga district of Chettinad where there is a famous Murugan temple called the Shanmughanathar Temple.

[14] A white sarong worn by Tamil men.

[15] A typically Tamil term of endearment for a girl, meaning, my dear.

[16] A mythical creature seen sculpted over pillars in many Hindu temples.

The image had stayed in her mind, like a painting that is forever etched on the walls of a cave: Appa standing with the morning light behind him, leaning with one shoulder against the old teak doors of the temple, in his white veshti, with a stray peacock feather he had picked up on the wayside tucked into his waistband. And even today when she thought of Murugan, that is how she imagined him—surrounded by the quiet solitude of dawn, pure, unadorned, solemn in his lonely communion with the universe.

And this is why Agasthya and her mother-in-law's way of worship made no sense to her—when Kartikeya was bedecked with strings of marigold and dressed in golden brocade, when the *odhuvaar*[17] sang, and the mridangam player's fingers beat out a rhythm in a rising crescendo, when the women dressed in gold and heavy silks, the *kumkum*[18] on their forehead trickling down in a rivulet in the sweating heat, when they queued up, flowers in hand at the temple door, meek, abject, ready to ask for a boon. Was that how your greatest moment of mysticism was supposed to be? Wasn't it when you were at your most glorious, awakened to all that is divine and consecrated within you?

That is why Vishnupriya disliked festivals. She'd much rather go in the quiet of the morning and stand in silent prayer in front of the little alcove where not too many devotees came, where Kartikeya was an unadorned medicant in search of truth.[19] Without knowing, Vishnupriya turned up her lips in disdain as she walked back home.

---

[17] The person who sings Tamil devotional songs from the Tirumurai at temples.

[18] Red turmeric powder used on the forehead.

[19] Refer to citation on Tank Road Temple on p.41.

Of course, it was exactly on one such day of high festivities which Vishnupriya detested that she had met Agasthya for the first time.

By then, she had already passed out as a topper from Raffles Girls', completed junior college and doctoral degree, managed to secure a job at the national labs for algorithm development and settled Appa's business debts with her salary. It gave her pleasure to see Appa stand surrounded by his friends in the open choultry of the Kundrakudi temple and declare, 'My Priya's maths? Always A+; she has the Chettiar brain for numbers, I tell you!'

They had returned to Kundrakudi that year, after nearly two decades, when, for once, her mother seemed happy with the kindly light that life seemed to be finally shining on her. After a lifetime of struggle with a husband who, unlike every Chettiar she knew, could never be successful in his business, Amma seemed happy. Happy with the kanjivaram in vermillion red that Vishnupriya had bought for her, with the way the old achi next door had admired her new gold bangles.

They had landed at Kundrakudi with the sole purpose of finding Vishnupriya, all of twenty-six by then, a groom. After running through the list of promising bachelors in Singapore, Amma and Appa had failed to find someone within the community who could match up to their daughter's qualifications. And so, Agasthya had walked into the picture—a software engineer, yet with his feet firmly grounded in Chettiar roots, nurtured by the wind and sun of their very own Kundrakudi.

That day it had been another day of Skanda Sasti celebrations. From the morning, it had been overcast. Under the gloomy sky, Vishnupriya had watched the preparations underway at the temple, the brass lamps that were lighted, the fire that rose in a searing orange flame, the pilasters with their vivid layers of bright colour that seemed to bear down on her just as they had done in her childhood, the yali's fierce claws that seemed ready to tear away flesh. The courtyard outside was being prepared as a battlefield, iron stakes chiseled in the village foundry being driven in with powerful blows of a hammer.[20] Even beyond, morning gradually turned to a scorching, relentless afternoon.

Agasthya and Vishnupriya had met away from all the commotion, on the banks of the Kundrakudi tank. By then it was early evening. There had been a brief downpour in the afternoon and the air had cooled down. The tank water rippled pale green, smooth as chiffon.

Vishupriya wore a saree. Amma had braided red oleanders in her hair, little pinwheels from Murugan's chariot. When Agasthya walked in, she noticed a man lean for the height he carried, with quick eyes that not only noticed everything, but also seemed keen to engage with all that they saw, a moustache thicker than Appa's over his upper lip.

Without much preamble, he had started talking about himself, the difficult life he and his mother had had after his father passed away young, how he got away from the village to study at Annamalai University.[21] If anything, unlike her own usually tongue-tied self, Vishnupriya had noticed the rather portentous way of speaking he had, as if he thought every word he uttered would go down in history. Yet today, when she thought of that evening, all she thought of was Shravanan. How

---

[20] This is done to re-enact the scene of battle between Lord Murugan and the demons.

[21] Founded in 1929 by a Chettiar entrepreneur in the Chidambaram district of Tamil Nadu, the university was established to assist students from economically impoverished families gain quality education and to promote Tamil literature.

was it possible that after all the miseries of his own childhood, Agasthya had so little empathy for his own son?

It was while they spoke that day in Kundrakudi that a young man whom Vishnupriya knew by sight had passed by. He had called out to Agasthya in a familiar way, '*Annan, romba naalachu parthu*, brother, long time since we saw you last!'

Agasthya had seemed inordinately pleased at being remembered. He'd waved at the man, and for a few seconds afterwards kept smiling to himself. Vishnupriya could imagine him going back home and telling his mother about the incident, both of them nodding in approval.

Difference number two, Vishnupriya had told herself. Unlike him, she hated being noticed and had always tried her best to blend in backstage.

It was at this point that a streak of white lightning had torn through the sky, illuminating in a flash the red flowers at the crown of flame trees. The winnowing wind had lifted Vishnupriya's dark curls, otherwise tied back in a severe braid, and suddenly she had noticed Agasthya look at her, as if seeing her for the first time. There had been something in those dark eyes of his that had made her groan inwardly, 'Oh God, do I have to contend with romance in a marriage of convenience as well?' she'd grumbled.

Yet the thought had made her pulse quicken, her heart miss a beat.

The marriage had taken place in Kundrakudi, and afterwards they had returned to Singapore. Vishnupriya thought of those early days when for a moment all they craved was union, and in the very next, only liberty, for union called to sacrifice too much of their different worlds. Those early mornings when Agasthya would come out from the shower smelling of Old Spice aftershave and stand in front of the TV, eagerly taking in all that was happening in India—the rise and fall of governments, disastrous earthquakes, celebrity breakups. She would watch him from a distance, notice the sparkle of the gold chain on his matted chest and return to her morning paper to catch up on Singapore news.

In those initial years, Vishnupriya had thought Singapore and India would not remain separate for too long, Kundrakudi and that magical evening by the chiffon green waters would work as a bridge. Within a year she had sponsored Agasthya's citizenship in Singapore and an extended permit to stay for Aathaa, her mother-in-law. They had moved to their new home in Tanah Merah.

Appa had been a regular visitor to their home then. Aathaa loved to hear him sing and her amiable father would happily sit on the divan, singing songs of Sundarar and Appar,[22] one after the other till he was lost in their words, completely immersed in their beauty.

But then, as the marriage moved beyond its fifth anniversary—and Vishnupriya crossed the threshold of thirty—his visits became rare for on every visit, Aathaa would bring up the topic of Vishnupriya not conceiving a child. 'Five years,' she would sigh, 'and yet there is no grandchild to play in our home. All she thinks of is office! Doesn't she realize that as a wife, giving a child to her husband is her duty? Is this what this blasted country teaches her, only to work, work and work?'

By the end of the sixth year, Appa would come only once, on the day of Pongal.[23] He would arrive bearing the gifts meant for a daughter's home—the brass pots of jaggery and sugar cane and turmeric plant—and sit on the divan, looking mildly apologetic.

---

[22] Sundarar and Appar are poets who wrote the musical hymns of the Tirumurai.

[23] A harvesting festival signifying an end of the old order and the beginning of the new.

Vishnupriya would watch Appa continue to laugh at what had been said, his eyes crinkling up because he knew if he stopped, the hurt would show.

It was Aathaa who had taught Vishnupriya to fast for Sasti[24] in the hopes of a son.

Every month, on the sixth night of the waxing moon, Vishnupriya would go to the Tank Road temple after office, having drunk nothing but water the entire day. In the evening after worship, she would eat a few slices of fruits. If for a few moments she would wonder what she was doing, standing in queue with the other women who had come to plead for boons, she would quickly brush the thought aside. For had not her parents always taught her that her first duty was towards her family? Singaporean or not, did not every Chettiar know that no sacrifice was too big when it came to the happiness of one's parents?

It was a relief when Shravanan finally arrived—as dark-eyed as his father, as sensitive to his family's wishes as his mother, as vulnerable in his need of their love.

For a few years, their home in Tanah Merah overflowed with happiness. Amma and Appa would come every weekend bearing gifts and play with their grandson. Vishnupriya would watch indulgently as Amma and Aathaa cooked together in the kitchen, made the idiyappams and thosai that Shravanan loved, made fish poriyal[25] but with very little chilli mixed into the curry powder. They would add tamarind juice to coax his taste buds, yellow ginger powder with its antiseptic qualities.

---

[24] This is a reference to the monthly day of Sasti. Refer to earlier citation on Skanda Sasti on p.45.
[25] Fried fish

But as they say, whatever life gives, it takes away in equal measure. And so, with time, they made some unsavoury discoveries about Shravanan—that he did not do as well in school as they expected, that he did not seem to have the acumen for numbers that every Chettiar was supposed to be born with. Amma had wailed, she had known the scourge would someday return to haunt her again. Aathaa had fallen silent, sat in front of her altar as if turned to stone. Agasthya had gradually distanced himself till he became one of those fathers whose only encounter with his son was a mutually disappointing one on the day of school results. And so, the years had passed till last evening, when Shravanan's school principal called with the news that he was not able to cope with his STEM subjects, that he would have to repeat the final year of secondary school.

'He'll not accompany me to the temple today,' Agasthya had burst out that morning. And even as Vishnupriya looked at him aghast, added, 'I find it embarrassing! I have friends there from Kundrakudi, engineers who studied with me in university. They ask questions!'

'We don't go to the temple to meet your friends, Agasthya; we go there to meet God.'

Vishnupriya had tried to keep her voice low so Shravanan would not hear from the next room; in the next room where her son sat sunk in a melancholic, monosyllabic listlessness, a child who flicks through a picture book without really seeing the pictures. She could see in her mind his room cast in darkness, curtains drawn till not a sliver of light entered, and wondered all the while if there were any forces on this earth that could protect her son, protect him from the final hurt of knowing that he had been awkwardly cast aside.

But in her heart, she had already known that there was nothing, no one to protect Shravanan, that Kundrakudi and that evening by the chiffon green waters could never work its magic, that Agasthya would never understand.

She entered the gates of her condominium. Christmas buntings were already up, a reindeer frozen in a joyous leap. She felt her feet drag; her atrophied mind no longer willing to grapple with the thought of what awaited her tonight.

It was Aathaa who silently opened the door for her. An uncanny silence resided in her home. The TV was turned off, the sofa looked as if it hadn't been occupied since morning.

Vishnupriya went to her own room. No one there either. With clammy fingers, she went through her sarees, took out the one she wanted to wear.

It was time. She needed to find Shravanan, have him get ready.

She walked across to his room. The door was locked, it did not budge under her fingers. For the last time she muttered the Skanda Sasti Kavacam, 'O son of Shiva, dweller of the heart, come daily to protect me.'

'Surprise!' The door flew open in her face. A grinning Shravanan stood, remote in hand, 'Amma, look! Appa helped me fix the LED lights in my room!'

She peered in. The room was flooded with light, one moment golden, the next a starry blue. One of the windows was open. A cool breeze blew in, lifting Vishnupriya's dark hair otherwise tied back in a severe braid.

Agasthya looked at her for a moment, then said, 'There was quite a storm in the afternoon. We were worried you wouldn't be able to get home in time.'

That evening, it was crowded in the temple. From long years of habit, Vishnupriya first went to the little alcove at the back where there were very few devotees. She stood for a few moments in silent prayer in front of Kartikeya, as he stood before her, wayfarer's staff in hand, a look of distant detachment in his eyes.

But then, she walked around to the main sanctum where Lord Murugan sat enthroned, nearly hidden under garlands of marigold, where the golden flame of brass lamps leapt into the air, losing themselves in whorls of dark smoke, where the odhuvaar's chanting was loud, and the mridangam player's fingers beat out a rhythm in a rising crescendo.

There was a sea of people here. Vishnupriya took her place among them, standing with her hands folded. The light from the lamps shone on the burnished gold of kanjivaram sarees, on the *kanakambaram*[26] flowers that the women wore in their hair, saffron in colour like a mendicant's robe. She prayed with all the mothers for the happiness of her son, her son who was born after two whole years of prayers, with a complexion that shimmered like blue luminescence in moonlight, with his father's unruly hair that no amount of coconut oil could tame. She prayed with the daughters for the health of her parents, with the wives for the long life of her husband. And as the mantra rose spontaneously, *O-m Sara-vana Bha-va, O-m Sara-vana Bha-va*, the colours, the seething emotions, the lights, and the music—all seemed to merge into a river of golden glaze.

Today, she saw no difference between seeker and the giver of boons.

---

[26] The 'fire-cracker' flower or the *Crossandra infundibuliformis*, which is orange in colour.

CHRISTIANITY

Gospel of John, 12:35

you are going to have the light just a little while longer.
walk while you have the light, before darkness overtakes you.
whoever walks in the dark does not know where they are going.

Christianity

Christian revelation places at its heart a mystical conjunction of opposites. And of this unity, Christ is the supreme example, for He is as much a Son of the Father as of the Mother. In acknowledging this, an essential part of Christ's nature is revealed: Christ fuses in his own being the highest 'masculine' understanding of the transcendent with the highest 'feminine' awareness of the beauty, nobility, and pathos of *this* life. The message of Christianity is a revolutionary one: that all of the world and its life must be transformed to mirror God's overwhelming love for mankind. The vision is unsparingly demanding: just as Christ offers his life and being in sacrifice, He demands of anyone who follows Him the same humility and self-donation. It is only with this selfless giving that the new beginnings, those real transformations into love, are made possible.

Eurasians

The Eurasians of Singapore are a small community with deep roots. In numbers, they make up a mere 0.4 per cent (about 17,000) of the population, and yet in spirit, they embody the very essence of Singapore: the East–West contact that was facilitated by the entrepôt status of SG which in turn influenced its economic progress, trade patterns, political doctrine and social ethos.

In one of the first interviews, a young community member speaks of the extreme energy that can lie in a fusion of the East and the West—the ancient wisdom of one with the modernity of the other. It's as illuminating as a starburst, as life-changing as a cosmic explosion. And this is exactly what the Eurasians embody as they pick out elements from the two worlds on either side (Portuguese, Dutch, English, Irish, Scots, and to a lesser extent Danish, French, German, Italian, and Spanish on one side and Burmese, Ceylonese, French Indo-Chinese, Indian, Malaccan, Malay, Cambodian as well as Macao and Hong Kong on the other), and weave it into an all-new tapestry, forge it into a consolidated third culture. It is in exploring this gestalt that Koffka's quote earns special resonance, 'It has been said, the whole is more than the sum of its parts. It is more correct to say, that the whole is something else than the sum of its parts.'

The community abounds with culture markers depicting the amazing singularity that can be achieved from this binary, or rather the smelting of this multiverse: Eurasian food that follows the spice trade in using lemongrass, turmeric, and fenugreek seed in pot roasts and stews, or the *branyo* dance that combines Portuguese folk with the Malay *ronggeng*. And so, there is the Eurasian family—egalitarian rather than hierarchical like those of the West, and yet thriving in the strength of family bonds and filial respect like those of the East. An interviewee describes the large family parties that they are accustomed to enjoying—yes, they might dance with their parents; but displaying those sexy, flirtatious moves of a rumba? No, sorry, that is a strict no-no!

So, in this world of melting and merging, are there no dividing lines? Well, an interviewee does speak of the unspoken social order of the Upper Ten vs the Lower Six. Thus, on one end of the spectrum are the elite, genealogically closer to their European ancestors, and on the other are those of Portuguese-Malaccan descent in whom European connections have become tenuous over time. Fortunately, the separation is not as black and white as it sounds. Inter-marriage and social mobility have ensured an easy mixing, and majority of the Eurasians inhabit the large middle-ground offered by the social continuum.

What emerges from here are the multi-layered memories. Nostalgia runs high in the lanes of Katong, that bygone seaside resort with holiday homes which, with the establishment of St Patrick's School and the Holy Family Church, increasingly turned into a Eurasian enclave.[1] Old residents speak of the milliners who provided feathered and flowered hats in latest Parisian fashion to the stylish Eurasian lady, the shell-pink taffeta dress with a trimming of blue flowers that they wore for a wedding, or the much-coveted Christmas party at Robinsons with marzipan fruits, cream buns and biscuits hand-iced in pastel shades.[2] But accompanying these are memories of a more local nature—the smell of the mosquito coil that drove away the unwelcome denizens of the Tropics, the 'dhuk' of the durian as the fruit fell from the tree on a silent night, or the many childhood afternoons spent playing in a neighbour's garden under the shade of the mango and the moringa trees.

But perhaps no treatise on the Eurasians of Singapore can be complete without mention of the Portuguese Malaccans, lasting evidence of genome that connects Singapore to Lusophone communities more than half a century old, from the time Afonso de Albuquerque moored his ships in the Strait of Malacca. This forms a rare, and as an interviewee confesses, more carefully preserved part of the heritage. It was the King of Portugal who had sent down men and women from a province in Portugal to reinforce the Portuguese population of Malacca, and this group—as they settled down in Tranquerah with their

---

[1] It was after World War I that Katong grew in popularity as a residential area. The foundation stone of the Holy Family Church was laid in 1922, and St Patrick's was established in 1933.

[2] In gathering these memories, apart from interviews, the books by Denyse Tessensohn (*Elvis Forever in Katong, Elvis Lives in Katong, Elvis Still Lives in Katong*) have been extremely helpful.

own language, culture, and cuisine—came to be known as the Kristangs. Today, the term Kristang is closely associated with the contact language that this community spoke, representing the unique Serani (Malay for Portuguese-Malaccan Christians, Serani meaning 'Nazarene') culture.[3] This 500-year-old Portuguese-Malay creole has seen an exciting revival since the 1990s when it was declared severely endangered by UNESCO, and as one explores such gems as the Kristang word *guru-guru* for dry rumbling thunder, *kachak* for betelnut cutter, or *lang-lang* for a thin, lanky person, one is overwhelmed not only by the lyricism of this language, but also perhaps the distinctive culture it represents—a worldview ever flavoured by joie de vivre, an enthusiastic embracing of the natural rhythms of life.

So, where do women stand in this community known for its unconventional capacity to straddle diversity and create a third culture that is robust enough to survive centuries? Reminiscences are replete with stories of families run by indomitable, betel-nut-chewing matriarchs, and not surprisingly, Eurasian women are a highly independent, resourceful group, encouraged to attain education and take up professional careers when women of other Asian communities were still sheltered. Perhaps it is a quality that stems from the insecurity of a colonized race's interface with the colonizer, but what it makes for are fascinating portraitures of tough decision-making women, highly adaptable and sensitive to picking up non-verbal cues. Names that come to mind are of Zena Tessensohn, who, with her sisters and friends, founded Singapore's first girls' sports club when she discovered women were denied entry to SRC (Singapore Recreation Club),

---

[3] It is to be noted that Kristang could still be heard in the 1970s in Singapore, particularly in Kampong Serani located near Haig Road.

or Hedwig Anuar who as Director of the National Library promoted local writing and Singapore's love for books.

And so, the Eurasians of Singapore have survived, with their love for Elvis' songs and for a wild diversity of food. They have never regained the glory of their pre-war days; large numbers have also emigrated. But at least a near-extinction of the Eurasian Association was averted in 1989, and since then, the community has been more conscious of its loss of place. For the gradual decline in numbers, older community members hold equally responsible the Ethnic Integration Policy of 1989,[4] the rapid urban development of Singapore as well as younger members who are allegedly less conscious of their communal identity than other communities. They speak of the trend to marry non-Eurasians when communal identity is happily surrendered to a broader Singaporean one. Yet, the hurt shows when multiple young interviewees mention that they, with their unique physical features—their 'throw-back'[5] eyes and maybe their Celtic bones—are often questioned about where they are from, whether they truly belong to Singapore. They justify their sense of being treated as outsiders by quoting statistics, proof that historically a larger proportion of Eurasians were local-born compared to their Chinese or Indian counterparts.[6] However, beyond the hurt and misunderstanding lies the

---

[4] For further details on Ethnic Integration Policy and how it affected the Eurasian community of Singapore, refer to *Singapore Eurasians: Memories, Hopes and Dreams*, ed. Myrna Braga-Blake, Ann Ebert-Oehlers and Alexius A Pereira, World Scientific, 2017.

[5] The term 'throw-back' is used in reference to the European features (coloured hair or eyes) that at times Eurasian children are born with. With genetic mutation and passing of generations, this is considered a rarity.

[6] The statistic shows that by 1931, 77 per cent of Singapore Eurasians were local born, a figure more than twice in proportion to the Chinese population, and five times that of the Indian community.

fact that in a country known for its migrant population, the Eurasians were the ones with Singaporean roots, that they hold within themselves the nucleus of change that birthed Singapore. Without them, the very essence of Singapore as the rider of the wind would be lost.

* * *

New Beginnings

Ruth (name changed), my mita or 'friend of new beginnings' has a strange, ephemeral quality, similar to what I think Cocteau means when he says 'being without being'. She is what fairy tales are made of—gossamer wings and fairy dust. You notice the smoky green eyes and your mind escapes to the olive trees of Tuscany, the way they turn silver in the sun.

What is it about her, you wonder, despite the familiar Singaporean accent? Just out of reach, like the glimpse of shade in a walled palazzo. And then, as your mind turns over her stories, you think of yet another woman: Will, older than Ruth by a generation and yet with the same quality of an assenting coexistence with the disorder of youth. There is no rigidity in sight, but just a consenting awareness of anarchy. As they dig into their past and pull out specimens with earth still clinging to their roots, you watch them grow, until they become a part of a boundless experience and the disorder doesn't bother you anymore.

And so, you bring them together as mother and daughter, though in reality, they merely belong to the same extended family of the kind common among Eurasians, with spreading maps of histories and geographies. And as you watch them interact against a dramatic set, you can see them change as life changes around them. For they are the evanescence of a dew drop, the chrysalis of a butterfly, you don't know at what moment of evolution you will catch them before they

assent to yet another new beginning, when the set will fold up and
they will move to yet another pageant.

Characters:

> *Wilhelmina ('Will' to family and friends): Mother*
> *Ruth: Daughter*
> *A security guard who comes and goes*
> *Ruth's father who makes a brief appearance*

Two women, one middle-aged and the other in her mid-
twenties sit in a porch overlooking Swan Lake Avenue.[7] It is the
wee hours of the night, the sky above them moves with the promise
of a storm, clouds casting them in inky darkness one moment,
and in the next, unveiling a thin, silvery moon. There is an old
breadfruit tree that stands to the left of the porch. Behind the
women is the silhouette of a house. It's fairly large, the drawing
room clearly visible under a single chandelier. Birthday buntings
are still festooned on the walls of the room, but otherwise, the
house stands dark and empty, windows shuttered, the party
obviously over.

> *Melody Gardot plays on a vinyl record in the drawing room:*

at the highest time of night nobody walks on this road
no one dares to come here, not even the dawn of day . . .

Ruth: What is it with you, the pioneer generation[8] types? Why
do you have to be so pushy? Why did you have to play Elvis's

---

[7] An estate with streets named after classical operas in Singapore.
[8] Refers to those who were sixteen and above in 1965, the year of Singapore's
independence.

songs today evening? It was my party! I mean, lol, who listens to Elvis nowadays?

Will: Oh, come on! What is so 'lol' about it? Elvis is our thing, he's—

Ruth: Mama! That's where you're wrong, he's no longer (holding up her fingers like a parrot's beak to denote quotation marks) our thing. He's a thing of the past, we don't listen to music like that. Music cannot be generic, it's so individual!

The watery moon shines on them for a moment, revealing Will to be a short woman with sturdy shoulders and thick ankles. She sits at the top of the short flight of stairs leading up the porch with her feet planted on a step below. Her hand is inside her skirt pocket where she holds something. Ruth is petite, with hair that comes down to her waist, wearing glasses which glint with an absent-minded intelligence. The moonlight also reveals the breadfruit tree and its tangled branches.

Will: But weren't you dancing to Elvis only the other day at Aunty Patricia's party, all you cousins, swooning into each other's arms? Everyone was talking about how they saw you dancing with your Cousin Simon all evening . . . (*stopping for a minute and whirling around to face Ruth, as if she has suddenly remembered*) And by the way, what makes you think (*holding up her fingers like quotation marks, imitating her daughter*) the pioneer generation is pushy—we're perfect, we change, we know, we reinvent ourselves! And I am not even pioneer generation; I turned fifty-five just last birthday!

Ruth: Mama, you've been fifty-five for the last five years! I'm so done with Elvis. (*Mimicking his rich baritone*) Can't help falling in love with you . . . I was dancing to Elvis only because Aunty Patricia had made sure she'd Aunty Patriciaed everything else out of the party. You guys need to remember this is no longer Katong, this is no longer Nana's house, that house was sold off thirty years back. (*Looking far into the distance, speaking in an undertone*) As Nana used to say, what are we without New Beginnings?[9] If it was not for New Beginnings, our world would have ended, what, maybe 2,000 years ago?

Will: (*with a sigh*): Ah yes Katong—those Shell[10] parties, those picnics on the beach with the *kelongs*[11] that would stretch right into the sea, those boys from St Pat's,[12] (*turning towards Ruth*) all this Marine Parade nonsense didn't exist then, you know?

Ruth: But Mama, that's the whole point. You need to move on. The Marine Parade 'nonsense' does exist now. This is our life, our world, we don't listen to Elvis anymore. This is the kind of music that is food for our soul, moody food of us that trade in love—

She points to the back, towards the vinyl. Gardot's voice is in the background:

nobody walks on this road, not a star, not a constellation
on this path that no one walks . . .

Will: Sweet Jesus! All these sad, sad songs, *andah-andah*[13] on a long, lonely road!

---

[9] The reference here is to the birth of Jesus. As Pope Francis points out regularly in his morning homily, it was Mother Mary's generous 'yes' that permitted God to take charge of history. Joseph who in trusting acceptance of what was to come, guided the Holy Family to safety. Without their acceptance of a new beginning, the Christian world would not have been shaped the way it was.

[10] Older Eurasians regularly reminisce about their work-life at Shell, the easy workday with a visit to the club in the evening.

[11] Malay word for a wooden offshore platform.

[12] St Patrick's School

[13] Kristang word for slowly walking or a stroll.

As if on cue, the nightjar that lives in the breadfruit tree lets out a long, melancholic call.

Will: What happened to all the romance of our time? Those red-blooded men, a Romeo at every street corner! (*She gets up, walking down, twirls around for a moment, as if dancing, but stops mid-way*) No wonder you are still unmarried at twenty-five!

Ruth: (*taken aback for a moment, then speaking in a more lively, conversational tone*) Well, maybe I'll just prove my friends right and finally marry a cousin![14] You saw, right, how my friends couldn't stop laughing, 'All you Eurasians are related lah! What, finally will you marry your brother?'

A cloud covers the moon again, casting a rippling shadow. Will cannot be seen anymore, only Ruth is visible on the staircase.

Ruth: (*after some thinking, when she sits with her fingers linked together around her knees*) Maybe finally I will marry a brother, given the way you and Papa can never approve of any of my boyfriends, and how Aunty Patricia has been patriciading all those boys in front of me all these years—Cousin Tom from Toronto, Cousin Simon from London, Harry from Timbuktu! (*She pauses again, continues, speaking more slowly, as if to herself.*) Emmanuel will never come back now, it's been too long, we've become too different, too far gone into things . . . He wanted so badly a life of devotion, the freedom of a life on the road, a downward mobility[15] that sets you free (*She addresses her mother*

---

[14] While it might not be exactly true to say a Eurasian marries their cousin, it is true that with the very large, extended Eurasian families of Singapore, youngsters do complain that virtually every Eurasian they know is related to them, and so, difficult to marry. This is also something that outsiders often joke about.

[15] The reference here is to the idea of 'the simple life' of poverty, chastity and obedience, considered to be the 'vowed' life, a longstanding tradition of Catholic religious orders like the Benedictines, Dominicans, and Franciscans,

loudly, directing herself towards the darkness) And Papa—why didn't he listen to me! Why did he order all that devil curry and feng and vindaloo[16] from the club today evening? All my friends wanted to eat was chicken rice and char kuay teow![17]

But midway through what Ruth is saying, Will dashes out of the shadows, moves eagerly to sit next to her daughter and puts an arm around her.

Will: Why don't you, darling? Why don't you marry one of your cousins? Go the Patricia way? Don't we owe it to our community? Why can't you be a little bit more like your sister, sweetheart?

Ruth: Because I can't, Mama. Because I find it hypocritical what my sister does—the way she happily wears the *kebaya*[18] to the club[19] and then changes into a *qipao*[20] for CNY, wears a dress to family get-togethers and keeps her off-shoulder blouses for the

---

and renewed again by St Ignatius who came centuries later. Here, they emulate Jesus who spent his adult life like a poor man. 'The son of man has nowhere to lay his head,' Jesus says in the Gospel of Luke, 9:58 or 'How hard it will be for those who have wealth to enter the Kingdom of God' in the Gospel of Mark 10:23.

[16] Reference to Eurasian food. Curry Devil is a fiery dish garnished with ginger, onion, chilli, and mustard seeds while vindaloo is from Goa. The feng is a milder stew traditionally made with pig offal.

[17] Typical Singaporean food—Hainanese chicken rice and char kuay teow, which is a Hokkien stir-fried dish.

[18] Upper garment worn with a sarong, typically by women of Southeast Asia or cheongsam is worn by Chinese women.

[19] The reference here is to the Eurasian Association of Singapore, though there is yet another establishment which shares the Eurasian heritage, the Singapore Recreation Club founded in 1883 by a group of thirty Eurasian men. Subsequently, the club has been opened to all the communities of Singapore, yet its original commitment to the promotion of all forms of sports remains unshaken.

[20] Also known as cheongsam, upper garment worn by Chinese women.

bar. Boots for that Christmas party, but no boots during Lent. It confuses me, I forget who I am!

Will: But that's who we are! We change, we adapt, we bend to the occasion.

Ruth: Well, I'm tired of bending! I can't do it anymore!

Will: You will have to, finally. You are right, Emmanuel will never come back. He's gone, he's joined the Church . . .

Ruth: (*barely appearing to listen*) Why did we stop going to the church, Mama? Do you remember our old church? St Ignatius,[21] where Nana used to take us? I really used to like it there, those long, silent retreats,[22] they gave me time to think, sort out things for myself.

Will: We stopped because of that Chinese boy at the vestry, the sacristan[23]—Emmanuel—whatever!

Ruth: He wanted to train to be a priest. That quiet, old-fashioned look he had . . . Why did Papa put down the phone when he called Mama? (*dreamily*) Why was Papa so eager to claim his pound of flesh? I wonder what his sufferance will be. You know,

---

[21] St Ignatius Church of King's Road, dedicated to Ignatian spirituality of the 16th century preached by soldier-turned-mystic St Ignatius, who founded the Catholic religious order, the Society of Jesus (the Jesuits). The underlying charism of the religious order is being contemplative in action, and so a Jesuit says, 'The road is our home.' They believe in 'incarnational spirituality' or that God may be found everywhere and in everything, even while they recognize the transcendence of God.

[22] In his seminal work, *The Spiritual Exercises*, St Ignatius of Loyola lays down the contents of a 28–30 day retreat designed for the participants to discern the will of God in their lives.

[23] Generally, a lay person who coordinates the worship services and is in charge of a sacristy.

whenever I used to meet him, I felt I stood on the edge of river, as if I was starting a timeless journey, as—

Will: (*cutting her short*) Move on, that's what you keep telling me, Ruth? That I'm too old, that I cling on too much. But it's you, darling, who needs to move on. (*raising her voice to make herself heard*) It's you, it's you. Don't you realize it's you who needs to?

They are interrupted by the crunch of footsteps in the distance. The security guard of the estate walks up the lane that stretches and bends a corner beyond the house. He walks on unsteady legs, bowed with arthritis and gout, over the heaps of dry leaves gathered on the kerb. He waves cheerfully to them.

Guard: You're out late today, Madam? Enjoying your music, I see . . . Nice, lively number, reminds me of my cha-cha club when I was young.

Ruth: (*sighing*) That's not cha-cha-cha, Uncle, that's jazz!

The guard doesn't hear, peers forward trying to read Ruth's lips. Ruth repeats herself, this time louder.

Guard: (*nodding his head knowingly*) Yes, yes, I know, it's late; you don't need to remind me, Miss Ruth. Goodnight, Madam! I have to go and do my rounds now, getting too old you know, slowing down. But management will not listen! Without you the estate will fall to bits, they say. If you are gone, who will take care of us?

Mother and daughter smile at each other, shaking their heads. They wave back to the guard, staring after his retreating back for a while.

Ruth: (*turning back to her mother*) I think I might have something to tell you, Mom.

Will: (*after searching her daughter's face rather worriedly*) Well, maybe there's something I might have to tell you, too.

> *She appears guilty, her hand has returned to her pocket.*
> *End of scene*

Will: I got my DNA test done (*pulls out a paper from her pocket, shows it to Ruth*)

Ruth: What! You of all people! I can't believe it. Did you get patriciaed into it? Something to add to your precious family tree?[24]

Will: No, no. Stop pulling Patricia into everything. That day in the wet market, when I went to buy chilli padi, you know, the day I wanted to make *sambal belacan*,[25] remember, you told me to make it extra spicy with the *grago*[26] from Portugal—

Ruth: (*impatiently*) Yes, yes, okay, the DNA test, you're saying . . .

Will: Oh yes. There was this woman with a lot of makeup on her face, I remember because she was sweating a lot and her pink foundation was melting—

> *Ruth clicks her tongue again impatiently.*

Will: Okay, okay, to cut a long story short, she asked me, 'You speak like a Singaporean, but you don't look like one. Where are you from?'

---

[24] Large Eurasian families are well-known for drawing up their family trees, sometimes going back four to six generations.

[25] Malay version of the sambal.

[26] Small shrimps

Ruth: But that's nothing new. We've been asked that before. You yourself told me when Nana was asked . . .

Will: Oh yes, my dear father, he used to sit in the balcony of our Katong house every evening—reclining like this on his favourite planter's chair, with his stengah[27] balanced on his tummy . . .

Ruth: Yes, yes, I know, that gorgeous house with all its silver bought from Nassim & Co,[28] its chaise lounges and lace antimacassars,[29] a prie-dieu in every bedroom, and Nana's Studebaker . . .

Will: (smiling at Ruth approvingly, warming up) And so your Nana was sitting, when in walks a gentleman[30]—in full silk suit and a hat, and Nana askes him as he usually did, all nice and polite, 'Hey man, so what's your poison?' But the man, instead of answering, says, 'I was noticing you in office today talking to the workers, so where are you really from?'

Will stops for a moment to look at Ruth to check for her reaction, then continues.

Will: My father, always cheeky! Too cheeky for his own good, if you ask me. Finally, couldn't keep his job down, couldn't keep his *ang moh*[31] bosses happy. So, he looks the man up and down

---

[27] From the Malay word for half, denoting a drink made of a half measure of whiskey and soda.

[28] Older members of the community mention the auction house Nassim & Co from where well-off Eurasian families bought their Austrian crystal, epergnes, silver, and furniture in Burmese teak.

[29] Small cloth coverings kept on the back and arms of sofas and armchairs.

[30] The Eurasians are famous for their skills of a raconteur and dislike being interrupted in between a good story.

[31] A pejorative term for white-skinned Westerners.

and says, 'Where am I from! Bloody burger, I thought this was my land till you walked in!'

Ruth: Yes, exactly. Isn't that exactly what you've told me always—that we're the originals, the others are the imposters. So, what made you do the DNA?

Will: I just thought it would be good to know (*shaking out her hair*) where do these glorious curls come from. And this magnificent nose—perfectly straight, see? (*Turning her profile*) It will remind you of the Romans.

Ruth: (*laughing despite herself*) So, what's the plan now? Travel to each country and tick boxes? Nose—aha, Roman (*gives an imaginary tick*). Skin colour—hmmm, going by the degree and shade—maybe Spanish? (*another tick*) You know how Papa is going to be angry if he hears this. He'll burst out in his good-ol' Eurasian way, 'What kind of horse piss is this, Will?'

Will: You know how we always knew that we are mostly Dutch-Burgher? Maybe just a little bit Iberian, mostly skewed towards Spain, with a healthy dash of Javanese-Melanesian? (*proffering the paper towards Ruth, and pointing at a line there*) Then where is this Chinese element coming from? Aren't we just mostly Dutch and that's why Papa named me after the Dutch queen?

Ruth: Wilhelmina—oh yeah! And all the *breudher*[32] that Aunty Patricia always bakes . . .

Both women pore over the paper.

Will: I've been thinking about it. The only Chinese person I can remember in our Katong house is Ah Lan—our Cantonese

---

[32] A traditional Sri Lankan Dutch-Burgher buttery yeast cake, baked in a fluted mould.

amah[33]. A lovely little thing, like a little porcelain doll in her black and white *sam-foo* and long pigtail. Do you remember her? When she passed away, Patricia and I cried buckets.

Ruth: I was just a couple of years old then, Mama; how'd I remember?

Will: Oh yes, of course. She could make the best lamb chops on this side of the Pacific. Very excitable—would throw up her hands and wail *beigkar fore*[34] for the smallest of things. A slight bit of extra salt in the chops—*beigkar fore!* The guy in the market is asking for a few extra cents for the bamboo shoots—*beigkar fore!* Papa used to invite his friends over just so that they could taste Ah Lan's cooking—her pot roasts and pies, the bread-n-butter puddings—uff! (She kisses her fingers and then stops short.) Do you think Papa named me Wilhelmina because of this Chinese connection? Wasn't Wilhelmina the Dutch ship that sailed to China? (*She stops short again, whirls around to Ruth.*) Do you think Papa and Ah Lan . . .

Ruth: Mama!

The sky has grown cloudier in the meantime, and there is a short sharp clap of thunder. The lightning shows up the fallen breadfruits that lie on the sidewalk and the knotted roots of the tree gnarled like a witch's finger.

Ruth: I can't believe I'm doing this. Sitting and watching you peel off layers like a *kueh lapis*[35]. Why do we have to take the test so seriously? Half the time they are fudged anyway!

---

[33] The amahs from Southern China would migrate to Singapore when times were difficult back home, often arriving when they were as young as twelve or thirteen and staying on for most of their lifetime in their employer's household.

[34] Cantonese word for disaster.

[35] An Indonesian rice flour pudding built up in layers, like a stack

Will: (*not paying any attention to Ruth, but looking at the paper*)
And what about this 15.7 per cent Portuguese? Why didn't
anyone ever tell me we had Portuguese blood?

Ruth shakes her head, sighing.

Will: I've been scrambling around for the last two days
thinking of all the Portuguese we used to know, and then
yesterday it struck me, Jesus Christ! Of course! How could I
forget? Poor Aunty Sara!

Ruth: Now who's this (*copying her mother*) 'Poor Aunty Sara'?

Will: You don't know her. Sara Frederica, she used to come
all the way from Kampong Serani[36] every Sunday to give us
catechism lessons. All of us kids knew about poor Aunty Sara
with her nine children and her good-for-nothing husband who
sang in a band and didn't bring home the bacon. The ladies of
Katong would do whatever they could for her—for some she
crocheted lace, for some she made *achar*[37]. I still remember one
day I went with Aunty Sara to get some Lourdes water from St
Joseph's Church[38], and she saw me looking at some St Pat's boys

---

[36] When the Dutch forces stationed in Singapore left at the end of World War
II, the Dutch Queen Wilhelmina and Dutch Queen Juliana camps in Haig
Road became home to a village known as Kampong Serani. In the 1950s,
an increasing number of Eurasians moved to live along Haig Road, in the
kampong. It had little wooden terrace houses set in rows along three sides of
a rectangle and the owner of the kampong lived on the fourth side and was
home to a large Portuguese-Malaccan Christian community.

[37] Pickle

[38] While the Catholics prefer to visit the Cathedral of the Good Shepherd,
the Eurasians also have a strong continuing presence at St Joseph's on Victoria
Street (closed for restoration since 2017). Founded in 1853, it has a neo-Gothic
architecture, interestingly adorned with Portuguese azulejos tiles and home to the
venerated Our Lady of Fatima. It used to have a parish largely made of Eurasians
of Portuguese descent.

and—'Alamah[39]! Don't look at them, Miss Will! You fall in love with one *kachoru algozu*[40], and you're doomed for life!' What a dressing down I got that day!

Ruth: (*who has been listening absent-mindedly*) So, are you done reminiscing? Can we go to bed now?

Will: Don't you get it? Maybe I am an adopted child—the unofficial tenth child of Sara Frederica, growing up in Katong. No wonder Aunty Sara would come, andah-andah, braving sun and rain every week to see her little *boneka*[41]! (*After some thought*) What if I'm adopted, Ruth? Maybe that's why Papa called me Wilhelmina—wasn't Kampong Serani built in the same barracks where Camp Wilhelmina used to be? Papa had served in the war, he'd know!

At this point a window opens upstairs, Ruth's father leans out in his night shirt.

Father: Can we have some quiet please? A man needs to earn his bread in the morning.

Ruth gets up to turn off the music. Gardot is silenced even as she sings the line:

on this path that no one takes, the highlight of my bliss—

End of scene

Ruth: (*standing at the top of the staircase and looking at Will who sits sunk in thought on one of the lower steps*) Mama please

---

[39] Interjection: 'Mother of God' in Kristang.

[40] Kachoru: Dog in Kristang; Algozu: Tramp, layabout in Kristang.

[41] Doll in Kristang.

quit it. Quit patriciacizing your mind, there's no gossip here, no conspiracy theory. Nana had told me before he passed away that he named you Wilhelmina because he wanted you to be a good, strong woman. He wanted me to be like you, was very proud of the name he'd thought up. And look at what you're doing, doubting everything the poor man ever did!

Will: But what if I *am* adopted? Maybe he never told anybody . . .

Ruth: Adopted? No, sorry! That temper of yours that sits so prettily on that Roman nose couldn't have come from anyone but Nana (*she laughs*).

Will: (*pulling herself together with effort*) You are right. Yes, for once, my daughter is right! My head was in the gutter that I was thinking all this. Thinking and thinking till I felt my head would burst.

Ruth: See, this is why I say it's dangerous to live in the past. It does things to your mind! (*sitting down next to Will, putting an arm around her shoulders*) So, should we retire for the night? As Romeo would've said, 'The night candles are burnt out, jocund day stands tiptoe on the mountain tops . . .'

Will: Wait, talking of Romeo, (*suspiciously*) weren't you going to tell me something as well?

Ruth: (*removing her arm from her mother's shoulder, looking away*) Yes, I know, isn't Romeo and Juliet such a great play? Romeo and Juliet and Friar Laurence and the royal mess they created between them?

Will: Friar Laurence? Oh no! Another friar!

Ruth: And the way Juliet didn't take a moment to decide between Paris and Romeo? That's how strong love should be.

Will: What are you even saying? Love and roses and candlelight! Pull yourself together girl, tell me what you wanted to say.

Ruth: Are you sure you can stomach it?

Will: We're Singaporeans, we can stomach anything!

Ruth: Okay, don't tell me I didn't warn you . . . (*saying in a rush*) I'm–planning–to–move–out–and–stay–on–my–own. (*Seeing her mother's mouth hanging open, she repeats more slowly.*) I'm planning to move out and stay on my own. I've already seen a tiny little place near work where I can move by next month.

Will: (*crumpling*) Oh *dekis*[42]! What kind of *diabu*[43] has got into you that you want to move. First your brother moved to Perth, then your sister married, and she is now so busy that she can never come and meet her parents. And now you!

Ruth: Mama, please!

Will: Don't you Mama-please me! (*pulling herself up to her full height*) What will people say? What is the need? Why did your Papa and I build this big house? (*pointing in the direction of the house*) Die, die, but must finish *lah*, otherwise where will children live?

Ruth: Mama don't you see, it's just not working out. All this Elvis songs and curry devil and Aunty Patricia is clouding up my mind. I don't know who I am, what I want to do!

Will: So, your only problem is with our traditions, is it?

Ruth: I feel I'm stuck in the middle of a maze; I don't know where to go after this . . .

Will: So you want to be all individual, is it? Generic doesn't work anymore for you.

Without their noticing, the moon of the early dawn has climbed to the high reaches of the sky. Silver light now slides off the fronds

---

[42] 'Oh dear' in Kristang
[43] 'Devil' in Kristang

*of potted palms. In the light, Swan Lake Avenue stretches before
them—rows of concrete houses, mostly identical.*

Will: It all has to be bespoke love and bespoke roses and bespoke
candles, is it? And with all that you'll set up your love nest, is it?

Ruth: No love nest, Mama. I just want to find out who I am.
Not the way you're doing it, playing the head, shoulder, knees,
and toes game—head from Rome, tick—shoulder from Greece,
tick. No, not that way—I want to know the whole of me. And
maybe to do that, I need to forget myself for a while. Move
away. You'll wait for me, won't you Mama? Like the father of
the Prodigal Son had waited every day for his child's return?

Will: Move away? Okay, move away, stay alone, forget all your
traditions. And then tomorrow, when you have children, what
will you pass on to them? What will you do? Give them bespoke
love and say 'Here, this is your culture', hand them a bespoke
candle and say 'Here, this is your heritage'? What will you give
them? What will live on after you?

Ruth: Can I tell you a little story?

Will groans, throwing her hands up in the air

Ruth: You remember how broken I was after Emmanuel left?
I used to feel so numb, as if I'd turned into a block of ice, an
iceberg floating in an unknown ocean. I'd just sit in front of a
mirror and stare at myself—heavy, sluggish, as if I had suddenly
grown a wooden head.

Will: (*aside*) You always had a wooden head, just like your father!

Ruth: And then, one day, Nana suggested I join one of the
retreats at St Ignatius, one of the ones on discernment[44]. He said

---

[44] The Jesuit training is all about a clear-headed, practical regimentation,
and as outlined by St Ignatius in his *The Spiritual Exercises*, 'discernment'

he was sure God would find me there, that this break-up with Emmanuel was just an excuse for Him to find me[45]. I miss Nana so much; I wish he was still here to tell me what to do . . .

Seeing Will look at her enquiringly, she speaks again.

Ruth: At the retreat, I had the strangest experience. They had sent us out to meditate in the rosary garden[46], but I couldn't. My mind was so full of Emmanuel, my breath was getting caught in my

---

lies at the heart of the Ignatian way of decision making as taught at a Jesuit retreat. Discernment of spirit helps one recognize the difference in one's feelings. According to Ignatius, when one feels a sense of joy, gratitude, and contentment, one knows one is moving towards God, and when one feels desolate and dry, that is when one is moving away from God. As in all traditions of Christianity, the basic desire is to move closer to God, and discernment is the tool chosen by St Ignatius for this.

[45] This is one of the key Ignatian principles that God meets people where they are. Ignatius himself was a vain man who wore his hair long and walked around in a flashy doublet and bright cap. Yet the surgery after Pamplona left him with a lifelong limp, and it was on his convalescing bed that he surrendered to God. He felt God had used his overweening pride for the good, for afterwards, he wanted to become a saint as good as St Francis or St Dominic. Since he himself had followed a circuitous route to God, he believed that God meets you where you are and as you are. He doesn't wait for one to stop sinning or to become more religious. Thus, in the New Testament, Jesus often calls people to conversation or meets them in the midst of their daily lives: while Peter mends his nets by the seashore or Matthew sits at his tax collector's office. The Ignatian model of discernment helps to reveal God's true desires for one and this is coeval with the Christian concept of Grace, i.e., the belief in the generosity and spontaneity of divine favour: 'Oh Lord, you have searched me and known me.' (Psalm 139)

[46] Praying the rosary is one of the oldest Catholic traditions from deep in the Middle Ages. A rosary garden is one set up like a rosary which forms a peaceful place for meditation and reflection. Designed to honour Mother Mary, stepping stones are placed instead of beads. One is supposed to say Hail Mary on the smaller stepping stones and Our Father on the larger ones, with the stones coming together to symbolize the decades of Christ's life. Just as the medallion of Mary is at the centre of the rosary, so also a statue of Mary forms

throat every time I thought of him. Plus, an MRT line was being built next door, and the construction work raised such a shindy. I tried and tried and yet couldn't concentrate, just went through the 'Hail Marys' and 'Our Fathers' like an automaton. And then as I was sitting under the statue of Mother Mary, a thought came to me—I realized that though Emmanuel was gone, everything we'd experienced together had stayed with me—the work we used to do at the dog shelter[47], the love and humility we had experienced there, our love for K-pop[48]. You know the way Emmanuel would always say our hybrid love was like K-pop, it would reach cult status one day . . . One day, Ruth, you wait and see, 'Friends, Romans and Pioneer Parents—we gather here to praise hybridity and all new beginnings and thoughts—not to bury it.'

Ruth laughs out loud. Turning around, she notices Will still sitting sunk in thought, scowling.

Ruth: Don't worry, Mama, just as Emmanuel has stayed on with me, I will also stay on, we will stay on. A little bit of you will stay and a little bit of Nana . . . and maybe a little bit of Aunt Patricia too (*looking at Will, trying to make her smile*). And even if I don't break into a *branjo*[49] every moment or don't ever eat a sugee cake[50] (*on an aside,* so bad for that waistline), what is in me will live on, and will find a safe shore in my children.

Will: (*not looking mollified, grumbles*) You mean, thanks to you, Eurasians will live only in spirit and not in person? We—

---

the heart of the rosary garden. There's a beautiful rosary garden at the King's Road church.

[47] This ties in with the Ignatian idea of downward mobility.

[48] K-pop is well known for the fusion of Eastern and Western elements.

[49] Branyo, a dance that combines Portuguese folk with the Malay ronggeng

[50] A Eurasian delicacy typically baked during Christmas

But she's interrupted as they hear a skittering among the dry leaves. It is the guard returning from his rounds. The first fingers of light touch the eastern sky, a light breeze blows lifting the leaves of the breadfruit tree. It appears tame, different from the night before.

Guard: I'll go home now, Madam; my shift is over, duty is done. I have to go all the way to Woodlands, you know, change two trains, then a feeder bus, and then at the very end of the road, after an uphill walk is my block. And then, *(as if he can see a vision)* my missus will be waiting at the door, the windows will be open, letting in the morning light. There'll be porridge with a bit of dried fish on the table . . . *(stopping short as if he has suddenly remembered)* Oh, did I tell you a young man had come looking for Ms Ruth the other day. I forget what is the name he mentioned—

Both Will and Ruth gather impatiently around him.

Guard: I'm really becoming forgetful nowadays, *bengong*[51], my missus calls me . . . Now, what was his name . . . David . . . or was it Adam . . .
Will: *(eagerly)* Was it with S—Simon?
Ruth: *(equally hopefully)* No, no, with E—Emmanuel?

Ruth twirls around, pulling an unwilling Will into the dance, singing 'Can't help falling in love with you . . .' while the guard stands scratching his head.

End of scene

---

[51] Malay for old and stupid

SIKHISM

Guru Nanak Dev Ji, *Guru Granth Sahib, 663*

yours is that Light which shines within everyone

Sikhism

Sikhism is a monotheistic faith born in the face of conflict, when the Islamic faith and Hinduism vied for control over Indian minds. As such, it has its roots firmly sunk in a syncretic affirmation of both religions, and, perhaps as a natural corollary, uses as its scaffold the twin ideas of interdependence and balance. For a seeker, Sikhism brings together in *sahaj* or easy equipoise the personal, social, and spiritual lives of a follower till no walls remain standing. In a process as natural as food cooked on a gentle fire, it is a seamless coming together of one's personal life impelled by the need to do an honest day's work (*kirat karo*), social life replete with the desire to seek welfare for all (*sab da bhala*), and spiritual life where the worshipper remains in ceaseless and equable connection with God or the finer self (*naam japo*). For a Sikh, the first point of departure and final point of return remain the words of the *Mul Mantar*, the Sikh's first prayer,

Ik Onkar/Sat Naam
There's only one God/Truth is His name.

Thus, it is truth that ensures the gradual coming together of matter and form, for the demolition of inner and outer embankments. It is with truth that a Sikh braces himself so his mind knows no despair[1]. It is on a quest for truth that Sikhism becomes an ever-joyous acknowledgment of the human body. It is the twine of gold beaten down and fired to absolute purity, the aquifer that keeps the farmlands green.

---

[1] Sikhism has an interesting concept of *chardi kala* or waxing mood of contentment which is achieved in the seamless unity of secular and spiritual aspects of life.

Sikhs

The Sikhs of Singapore are around 12,000 strength and are a minority within minority status, subsumed in the racial category of Indians, and yet a community that maintains a distinct identity. The lasting impression the Sikh guardsman or the proverbial *jaga* left on Southeast Asian imagination is evident in the figurines discovered in 2011 at the Bukit Brown Cemetery. These tall, sinewy figures of yore with curly moustache and firearms, proudly standing guard over Chinese graves, bear lasting testimony to the new identity the Sikhs forged in their country of migration—figures of valour and unflinching loyalty who could be trusted to stand by in life as in death.

It was in 1881 that Sikhs arrived in large numbers from the British-Indian province of Punjab as part of a new police contingent. By then, the British army recruitment policies were in place, assigning to the Sikhs a place on the martial race construct. This is perhaps ironic because long before, in 1850, yet another Sikh had arrived on the shores of Singapore—Bhai Maharaj Singh—the mythical, swashbuckling rebel on a black steed, the revered Guru and saint whose portrait Lord Dalhousie kept as a trophy, and of whom Henry Vansittart, Governor-General of Jallandhar, wrote, 'The Guru is no ordinary man, he is to the natives what Jesus was to the most zealous of Christians.' Bhai Maharaj, with a formidable guerrilla network across Punjab, the phantom rider who needed nothing more than an audacious battle-cry blown on a conch shell to call his men to action, arrived in Singapore, chained and shackled, a prisoner of the British, to spend his last days at the Outram Prison. He was the last of the rebels of the Anglo–Sikh Wars, a protector of the Sikh Empire, the last domain to fall before British control had the Indian subcontinent in a chokehold.

Perhaps it was the invisibility of Bhai Maharaj that wielded more power on British imagination than a man with a garrison ever could, and it was to destroy this that they brought him to Singapore. Yet he continued to rule. Even after an inglorious death, his vision clouded by cataract, a cancerous sore on his tongue, today his tomb at the Silat Road Sikh Temple is where pilgrims gather.

What Bhai Maharaj represents is the militarization of Sikhism, the tradition of Khalsa Panth propagated by Guru Gobind Singh, the tenth and last Guru of the Sikhs. It is a way of life for the righteous soldier, the saint-warrior who fights not for personal power, but to establish the *Halemi Raj* or sovereignty that has divine sanction, based on justice for all. It is this idea of wider good for a larger people rooted in religiosity that inspired the Nobel Laureate Rabindranath Tagore. He sought in Sikhism an alternate roadmap to nationalism, different to the exploitative one taught by Western colonizers, writing,

> On the banks of the five rivers
> The Sikhs awaken today to the voice of saints
> Fearless, they know no mercy to themselves
> A thousand voices raised in prayer
> That shake the earth to its very foundations[2]

The connecting link between the two stories of the worthy rebel, Bhai Maharaj Singh and the humbler jaga of Southeast Asian lore, is the concept of *miri* and *piri* taught by Guru Hargobind, the sixth of the Sikh gurus. At the time of his coronation, the Guru had asked to be donned with two *kirpans* or swords—the miri as a symbol of temporal authority, and the

---

[2] From 'Bandi Bir' or 'Captive Warrior', a poem by Rabindranath Tagore

piri as a symbol of spiritual authority. Ever since, miri and piri have become the ultimate images for the syncretic unity that Sikhism represents wherein the sword is a metaphor for God, delicately balanced at an intersection of state power and spiritual power. Thus, Bhai Maharaj was a saint-soldier: the soldier in him never allowed him to sleep, and the saint never allowed him to oppress. And similarly, when the jaga picked up his weapon, he did so to protect the vulnerable in a perfect balance of spiritual and temporal powers. Sikhism is all about this syncretic coming together of the everyday with the transcendental, and with this gradual disciplining of the mind and body, the devotee very naturally moves forward on his path of worship. It is a dismantling of walls, an opening of the sluice gates; and nothing can stop his progress as long as his quest in both his secular and spiritual lives remain one and the same—truth, a word that is synonymous with God for the average Sikh.

But how does a faith that was born in a village in India (now in Pakistan), in the face of conflict with the Mughal Empire, one whose sense of military and missionary zeal was sharpened during the Anglo–Sikh Wars, remain relevant to modern-day Singapore? How does a faith that taught a syncretic unity first among the simple yeoman cultivator not lose its way in the urban jungle that demands multiple life-worlds and an almost schizophrenic creativity to remain relevant? For relevant it is in Singapore, with seven gurdwaras (two recognized by the government, five registered as *sabhas* as they represent regional and not communal interest) as well as a handful of socio-cultural bodies which work cohesively for the welfare of the community. Today, they aim to be a model community, contributing to Singapore at large, but also careful of their own legacy, and a learning of the Punjabi language that the NTIL (Non-Tamil Indian Language) policy allows.

A question about relevance invariably leads to the central idea of *seva* or selfless service that runs through Sikhism. If a male interviewee mentions the Sikh Gurus who travelled across borders tending to the sick and providing for the poor at times of natural disasters, and connects it to the charity work done by the Singapore gurdwaras during the 2020 pandemic, then a female interviewee speaks of the Night of Giving organized by the women of the Khalsa Association. In addition are names dotting Singapore history—Bhopinder Singh who worked selflessly during the SARS outbreak, and Balbir Singh who worked with children afflicted by the Down Syndrome. It is a community that keeps its *langar*[3] (community kitchen) open to migrant construction workers and domestic helpers even if it comes at the cost of a dwindling number of regular/expat worshippers visiting the gurdwaras.

Now, where do women fit into this faith, given obviously to warrior tradition? It is true that they are often the mainstay of strength in their homes, the 'Kaurs' or princesses who do not change their names even after marriage. But it is also true that female role models are few in Sikh mythology. If there is a Bebe Nanaki[4] or a Mata Gujari[5], then they are better acknowledged in their traditional roles of sister or mother to the Sikh Gurus, women who helped discern the paths the Gurus

---

[3] The community kitchen is a unique embodiment of the concept of *miri* in Sikhism with its emphasis on maintaining a healthy body for a perusal of the spiritual path.

[4] Sister of Guru Nanak ji, the first Guru; she was the first to realize her brother's inclination towards spirituality and encouraged him to use music as a tool to serve God.

[5] Mother of Guru Gobind Singh and wife of Guru Tegh Bahadur, the ninth Guru; as legend goes, it was Mata Gujari who advised Guru Gobind Singh to add the sweet *batase* to the holy water at the time of the initiation of the *Panj Pyare* to Khalsa Panth, thus underlining their path of military zeal with ideas of compassion and empathy.

crafted, yet remained as shadowy lieutenants themselves. And while the faith does speak of the unity of the human spirit, the sociological reality is the influence on the earlier generations of the male-dominant North-Indian culture. Gender difference persisted, as did a sinuous caste system, with the Khatris at the upper end, the Aroras as the mercantile class, etc.

However, what is interesting to note is how, in the course of three generations, the world of the women has widened. If for the first generation of Sikh women the point of reference was her village in Punjab and for the second the Sikh-Punjabi society of Singapore, then for the third it is the wider Singaporean community, in all the multicultural complexity and inner calibration that it demands. With a woman's usual astuteness, an interviewee says, 'When a woman chooses her husband today, she often places the freedom she will get in his household at a higher priority than his caste or social background,'—prudent wisdom obviously born of past experience.

* * *

Chickpeas to Cook

I look at Mita, my 'friend of the aquifer', in her pink Punjabi suit and pearls. Blush of lipstick. The evening draws itself out in broad swathes of vermillion. It is a landscape drawn in a child's hand, a tree where nesting birds return, a hut with a conical roof. I wonder why sitting before her, after meeting many others of the community, I feel this is where all the paths of life lead. This is where daughters are raised, grandchildren are born. Beyond this, there is no confusion; beyond this, the line stretches, a single linearity that touches on its course points where the artist makes his presence felt far more strongly than the model.

She speaks to me of her father, how he taught her to differentiate between form and matter, flits for a moment to the words of the Mul Mantar, mentions the shrine of Bhai in Singapore. I scramble after her. What is the twine of gold that connects the dots?

She speaks of the three tenets of Sikhism; the rabab, the instrument of the Sikhs. It is fretless, she says, all you need is intuition to pluck at its strings. I continue to blink; the simplicity of the line that I noticed at first seems to have disappeared. I wonder if she is leading me deeper into the cave or out of it?

Mita smiles, turns to her personal life. She speaks of how, at a critical juncture of her life, she had consoled her father, taught him to distinguish between form and matter again.

And suddenly I see light. Of course! It is truth that is the underlying thread of gold, beaten down, purified in fire. I think of Kabir's doha, it is not enough to spout truths, truth needs to reside in your heart. For truth is the aquifer that keeps the farmlands green. Above is the landscape drawn in a child's hand, a plain of no walls, bathed in silver moonlight. Truth is the only matter, all else is form. There is no confusion there, all you need is good intuition.

It was the aquifer that kept the farmlands green. In Bujrur—where land is fertile and all day long parrots squawk in mango trees; where after Baisakhi[6], when the new maize is sown, I felt I walked on green-grass clouds, swaying fields that turned into a misty blue in the distant horizon, till I couldn't make out if I walked on land or over the sky; where one day, while the clouds cast gently-shifting shadows at my feet, and the dappled pathways held enough magic to dazzle my eyes—I walked straight into Bhagwan Dada's tank. I had heard the *klup-klup* of his spade on quiet afternoons, but had not realized that the basin

---

[6] The spring harvest festival of Punjab

of water that he had dug for watering his land ran so deep. And
so, I tumbled through the green sludge and whirling sand and
the bits of root that had been chopped off the old banyan tree.
I felt the water enter me—the green and blue and the golden
coins of light with a bit of Bujrur in them, and I did not really
mind. I had not realized it was so cold down below, so inky
black . . . until, suddenly, a pair of strong arms were under me,
a flash of warm sunlight on my face.

I lie in my bed for a moment. Dawn is yet to break outside my
window. Smoke from a charcoal fire floats in. Bebe is lighting
the clay oven in the kitchen; soon black lentils will be bubbling
on a slow fire. That is Papaji plucking the strings of his rebab[7],
the first notes of the morning. Bebe will soon scream, 'Do you
have nothing better to do, *nikamma*[8]?'

But then I wake up with a jolt. No, no, no—that is all wrong!
Today is 24 October, Bhai's birthday, and I'm in Singapore. I
have so much to do—the chickpeas to cook, my Punjabi suit
to iron so I can wear it to the gurdwara. But then, before that, I
need to feed Miri and Piri. Poor Miri is full-term pregnant, ready
to birth her litter any moment. She gets so hungry! And that
is not Papaji on his rebab. That is Baljit, my husband, snoring
softly as his sleep gets lighter. Any moment he will awake and
ask for his first cup of chai. Breakfast will need to be made before
my children—my sons and daughters-in-law—leave for work. I
had put in an advertisement for Bhai in the Straits Times some
days back, as I have done every year for the last forty odd years.
A small pile of letters lies on my desk, ready to be opened and

---

[7] A fretless instrument of the Sikhs, adopted from the Muslim court musicians
of Kabul

[8] One who does not do any useful work

read. And to top it all, today the girl from the archives is coming to interview me for her book, about all the work I have done for the Khalsa Association of Singapore and the Punjabi School all my life.

I groan silently. Could it get any worse?

The girl, when she arrives, seems nice enough, though obviously a bit disorganized. I watch her struggle with her laptop and umbrella for a moment before I take them from her hand. I walk her straight to the kitchen, I do not have a minute to lose today. I have already set up a small worktable there for her.

She stops for a minute to look at the climbing frame we have made from hemp rope for Miri and Piri. This is where they sharpen their claws, working off their excess energy. Now, Miri sleeps, curled in her basket, replete with her early morning bowl of milk and the Marie biscuits I have given her.

In the kitchen, golden mustard oil burbles, silver juliennes of onion turn shell-pink. Black cardamoms lie open on the countertop, as bristly as the bark of a tree, as fragrant as a forest grove after rain. Chickpeas made in Punjabi fashion had always been Bhai's favourite dish, and I have made it every year for his birthday, every year since he . . .

I have already boiled the chickpeas, with salt and a spoon of tealeaves tied in muslin. The salt will soften the chickpeas till their skin splits; the tealeaves give them a nice mature colour. It is only afterwards that the pea will be ready to cook in its curry.

I see the girl stare in amazement at the *kadhai*[9]—made of glistening brass, big enough to feed at least a platoon. It was my mother's, brought here all the way from Bujrur. Nowadays,

---

[9] A bowl-shaped pot with handles on either side, used in Indian cooking.

it comes in handy when I cook *mee goreng*[10] for my family. She turns to look at the heavy *okhal moosal*[11] that I have dragged out today. It is dusty under a fine net of cobwebs. Bebe would grind her whole spices in it.

'My mother used to say that it's only when spices come under the stone pestle that they release their oils, become more flavourful,' I explain to the girl.

It is still early morning. Sunrays fall on the mossy bole of the jackfruit tree outside, casting the kitchen in a pale green light. My early morning dream has stayed with me, the day I had fallen into our neighbour's tank in Bujrur, and Bhai had pulled me out in the nick of time, before I hit rock bottom.

Papaji had looked at me as I lay spluttering by the tank, '*Gudiya*[12], why didn't you scream, swim up to the surface, shout for help?' But I had merely stared back for I did not know the answer to that question.

'We used to stay in Bujrur village,' I tell my interviewer. 'Near Anandpur Sahib, and every year, we'd go over to Anandpur to watch the *jaloos*,[13] the *nihangs*[14] riding their twin horses,

---

[10] An Indonesian-style fried noodle dish.

[11] Mortar and pestle.

[12] Doll, a term of endearment.

[13] Procession

[14] An armed Sikh warrior order, dressed in blue, and believed to have been founded by Guru Gobind Singh. The reference here is to the annual Hola Mahalla festival held in Anandpur Sahib of Ropar District. The festival is an occasion for Sikhs to demonstrate their martial skills. It was in Anandpur Sahib that Guru Gobind Singh founded the Khalsa Panth, the order of the saint-soldier, in 1699. It was also here that the Battles of Anandpur were fought in which Mata Gujari and the two sons of Guru Gobind Singh were taken captive and killed by the Mughals. Incidentally, it was Guru Gobind Singh who selected the Guru Granth Sahib, the central religious text of the Sikhs, to be his successor. There were no more gurus after him

brandishing swords. Though, of course, we didn't stay in Bajrur for too long.'

No, we—Bebe and Papaji, and my eleven siblings—we'd moved to Singapore soon after. Papaji had wanted to join the police band of Singapore; his friend had told him life was good in this island-city.

But first we travelled to Delhi in search of an agent who could get us our passage on the ship, and it was there that the incident happened. The incident that made Papaji stare at me as if he had not seen a stranger child before, and me to stare back, unable to find an answer, all over again.

I remember that in Delhi we had gone to visit the Sis Ganj Sahib Gurdwara[15] in the old part of the city. Even as I had walked in, I had been struck by its beauty, its spreading pavilions and parapets, and walls made of sandstone that trapped the sunlight. Yet those walls told one of the saddest stories of the Sikhs. We had listened enthralled as Papaji told us about Guru Tegh Bahadur Singh, the poet and soldier, beheaded by the Mughals.

'It was under this tree that our Guru lost his life,' Papaji had pointed. He had shown us the well from which the Guru had drawn water, the last drops to quench his thirst before his martyrdom.

Later, I had wandered off to the main sanctum where the rebab played and the *ragis*[16] sang, '*Tegh Bahadur Simriye/Ghar*

---

[15] The word 'Sis' means head. Sis Ganj Sahib Gurdwara is located near the Red Fort and Jama Masjid of Old Delhi and is the site of Guru Tegh Bahadur Singh's martyrdom. It was here that the Guru was beheaded on the orders of Aurangzeb. On India's Republic Day, the Sikh Regiment of the Indian Army salutes the Gurdwara after saluting the President of the country.

[16] A Sikh musician who plays hymns (*shabads*) in different ragas at the gurdwara

Navnidhi aave dhaaye[17].' The music mesmerized me, seemed to draw me to a remote world where I did not hear Bebe's cries to come and eat lunch, or Papaji telling us to stay together in a strange city. I stood and listened to the notes, wading into their quiet solemnity, feeling my mind go silent, my heart slow down.

I was told later that a priest from the temple had found me, and asked me where my father was. Yet, I kept quiet, something inside me seemed to hold me back; I just couldn't find an answer.

Papaji had asked me later after they found me, 'Why didn't you answer, *puttar*[18]? Why didn't you tell *Gyaniji*[19] my name?' I had simply stared back, feeling slightly guilty that I had let Papaji down.

'Bebe had, of course, been very angry. "Girls should not have such wandering feet," she had shouted,' I tell my interviewer. 'She was always like that, you know.'

My mother had shouted so much that after a while I felt my ear drums would burst. I would have started crying if it was not for Bhai—my brother, elder to me by two years. I had seen the relief that flooded his eyes when he saw me, like the sun sparkling on a grey ocean, and that look kept me going.

My interviewer looks at me intently over her reading glasses. I can see the questions buzzing in her head, 'Was I an unloved girl child, discriminated against, maybe abused by my parents?'

---

[17] The lines mean 'Meditate on Guru Tegh Bahadur Singh so the nine spiritual gems are bestowed on you.' Here the reference is to Guru Tegh Bahadur who was a poet and scholar, to whom is attributed 115 of the hymns included in the Guru Granth Sahib. It is believed that meditating on his name brings the spiritual treasures of faith, absorption, contentment, ecstasy, etc. to the devotee. Simriye is from the word 'Simran', a beautiful concept of Sikhism meaning 'to stay in touch with the divine self or with the finer self within'.

[18] Child, a term of endearment.

[19] Someone with spiritual knowledge who can help the congregation in understanding the sacred texts and the history of the religion.

But then she changes her mind, possibly stores the question away to ask later, at a more opportune moment. She asks instead, 'So tell me about your journey to Singapore, Mrs Kaur.'

Ah the journey! Can these girls, with probably a luxury cruise or two under their belts, even imagine what it was like being holed up in the lower deck for so many days? All thirteen of us, seasick, barely sleeping at night. Papaji had to tie the little ones down so that they would not slither off on the deck, slippery as it was with seawater and oil.

'Bebe had got her kitchen utensils with her, in a big gunny sack, all this brassware that you see,' I reply in answer to her question. 'But of course, it was so turbulent, we could barely cook. We survived on *panjeeri*[20] for all those days.'

'*Panjeeri*? Some kind of a punch . . .' the girl ventures, her eyes rounded with surprise.

'No, no,' I cannot help laughing. 'It's a dish that pregnant women eat so they stay healthy.' Yes, *panjeeri* is what we had eaten all those days, so much so that during the three pregnancies of my own, I could not force myself to eat even a spoonful.

Yet all through the difficult journey, our Guru, Tegh Bahadur Singh, kept me company. All I needed to do was to close my eyes and visions of the gurdwara would come back—the harmonium playing, the solemn voice of the ragis singing, the sandstone walls which glowed with the fierce summer sun and yet held a strange peace.

'But you know, once we reached Singapore, something rather strange happened.'

It was one of those rare weekends when Papaji had got his pay and taken us for a movie. In the movie was a character of a Sikh—on a horse, galloping into battle. He looked a bit like our

---

[20] A mix of whole wheat, nuts, and seeds in ghee, eaten by new mothers

Guru, Tegh Bahadur Singh, with the same large, calm eyes. And yet, in his hand was an unsheathed sword, dripping with blood. And every time he appeared on the screen, everyone laughed, for he was the comic relief, the sardar who was always impulsive and foolish! I remember I had turned to ask Papaji what it was that the moviemakers wanted to show—the courage of the Sikhs, or was it his swagger, or even worse, a witless foolhardiness?

'You tell us about our gurus, saint-soldiers, brave and sacrificing. And yet why do these movies always show the Sikhs as such figures of fun, rushing into battle without thought?' I had asked, and in answer, Papaji had told me something that would return to me again and again at the worst times of my life, at those moments when I desperately needed to chase away the shadows:

'Puttar, we know what is in our heart, *mere Guruji nu patha mera dil di baat*[21]. What does it matter what people say?'

And so, we had arrived in Singapore after being quarantined at St John's Island. The police quarters were in Thomson Road, a stretch of rectangular space with a zinc roof that we called our own. We would cook there by day, and move away everything to roll out our mattresses by night. Even as we fell asleep, Papaji would remain outside, just outside our door in the little sit-out. In the darkness, he would look up at the stars and strike up a note on his rebab.

'Papaji missed Bujrur, you know. But he was still happy, happy that he could send us to English schools.'

I say this, but in my mind's eyes, I see Bebe shouting at Papaji, 'Why do girls have to go to school? Why can't they

---

[21] 'The Guru who sits within me, knows the words of my heart.' A beautiful concept of Sikhism implying that the Guru, or the divine self, is within each one of us. The journey of a Sikh is to finally unite with the Guru or one's own divine self.

just stay at home and learn cooking? That's all they will finally have to do!'

But Papaji was adamant, and we were admitted—me and my four sisters—to the Lee Kuo Chuan Primary School in Thomson Road, just opposite the Police Academy. Of course, Bebe would have none of the English style at home. The set rule was that we girls would return from school and fold away our uniforms; she did not like us to wear anything but Punjabi suits at home. In fact, my uniform was the only skirt I ever possessed in my life.

'As the eldest daughter of the family, it was my duty to cook, and so I'd return from school and walk straight into the kitchen and stay in there all evening.'

I watch my interviewer fiddle with her recorder, trying to reset it. I think she does not know how to handle such confidences, old reminisces from the past. Or is she moved by my story?

I turn back to my cooking, bringing my mind back from the past with difficulty. The sun by now is a sharpened gold, dividing the backyard into clear zones of light and shadow. The fire is flaring up, the chickpeas make an inordinate amount of noise, spluttering and rising to the surface, bursting with angry pops in the curry. I bend down to lower the flame of the gas.

My mind goes back to Bhai, whose birthday it is today. I can see the pile of letters, replies to the advertisement I had put out in the newspaper, sitting on my desk. They need to be looked through. Maybe finally I will have an answer to the questions that have plagued me all these years, questions about Bhai . . .

All through those difficult years, Bhai was my greatest support, my best friend. We barely needed any words; we would look at each other and quick telegraphic messages would skitter between our eyes. I know even if we meet today, he will call out, 'So, was the bus crowded?' and the two of us will burst out laughing. Bhai's eyes will sparkle with the fun of it, and those around us will wonder, 'what is wrong with these two oldies?'

Nobody will understand we are referring to those evenings when the two of us would return walking from school because we had spent the few cents of bus fare on *chee chong fun*[22] from the man with his baskets on a bamboo pole. And as we entered home, Bebe would exclaim, '*Arre*, why are you so late today? Was the bus very crowded?' And the two of us would vigorously nod our heads, not daring to talk, laughter and excitement flowing like electricity in our veins as we looked into each other's eyes.

But unfortunately, over the years, laughter and happiness seemed to drain away from our house. With eleven children, Papaji found it increasingly difficult to manage with his salary from the police band. Bebe was getting more and more insistent that we girls stop studying, that Papaji should not take on the extra burden of our school fees, it would serve no purpose anyway. And on top of everything, Bhai's health slowly started going downhill. I would see the swathes of shadow under his eyes, like tire marks on a wet road, his sudden nervous energy, the long periods sunken in listless silence. Bebe, Papaji and I, each one of us would notice, but we would not talk about it for fear our worries take on the shape of reality.

And then that evening . . .

I was in my final year of secondary school. Bhai had already won a scholarship to the university. That evening he returned from a Khalsa Association match[23], a map of sweat on his back,

---

[22] Cantonese steamed rice rolls

[23] The erstwhile Singapore Sikhs' Cricket Club became the Singapore Khalsa Association and ventured into a range of sports including hockey, badminton, kabbadi, golf, and netball for girls.

his hockey shoes flung over his shoulder. I was in the kitchen, and with my A-level exams just a week away, I had my English text propped up next to the stove, trying my best to study while I rolled out the *rotiyan*[24].

Bhai had come in and burst out, 'Bebe, she is cooking again?'

'Yes, your Papaji wants to have early dinner. Why, are you hungry?'

'Bebe, she has her exams!'

'So?'

I had turned around to look from the stove—Bebe momentarily taken aback by the genuine anger she saw in her son's eyes. But she had recovered fast, turning to Papaji in her appeal for justice, '*Suno, ab*[25] we can't even ask our children to do housework!'

And then she had turned back to Bhai with renewed vigour, 'And you! May I ask Your Highness, where have you been till so late? The match was supposed to end at four!'

I had felt my trepidation rise. I had caught myself snatching a prayer, saying as much of it as I was able. No, no, no . . . Bebe should not go near Bhai.

But she had. She had moved close to Bhai, drawn herself to her full height, and glared into his bloodshot eyes, brought her face as close as possible to Bhai's face and sniffed his breath.

And in a moment when the world seemed to halt to draw a shaky breath, I had heard the resounding slap, the tremor in Bebe's voice as she hissed, 'Tell me, what is the vile stuff you've taken that you are talking to your mother like this?'

As if in slow motion, Bhai had staggered towards the wall, crumpled against it like a ragdoll. I had seen his balled-up fist

---

[24] Roti (Indian Flat Bread).
[25] Listen, now.

hit against the wall, again and again, his *kara*[26] making marks—deeper and deeper—like the ones a prisoner makes in his cell in desperate anger.

By then tears had poured down Bebe's cheeks, remorse writ large at what she had brought on. She turned back to Papaji, her voice high-pitched, '*Sadde munde theek, horan de kharab,* my child is good, it's the others who have turned bad. What did I do? Why didn't you stop me?'

But Papaji had not replied. He had merely slumped down in silence. In fact, after that, all I heard in our house was silence—Bhai's unforgiving silence towards Bebe, Papaji's unforgiving silence towards himself. And the marks of the *kara* remained on the wall, like the watermark of a past deluge.

I had known all along that Bhai could not do anything wrong, that his problem lay elsewhere. But we were still living in the police quarters then, in Thomson Road. The band, those fifteen–twenty families of us, was a compact unit, and word travelled fast. Tongues soon started wagging about Papaji—that he could never control his wife, and now he had lost control of his children as well, that his daughter was of a marriageable age and yet wore a skirt and went to school, and now his son was going to the dogs, too; that Papaji had always been a nikamma, now he had become a *nakara*[27] too, not raising a finger to do anything about the situation.

'And as misfortune never comes alone, on top of everything, this was the time when Papaji was about to retire,' I tell my

---

[26] The steel or cast-iron bangle worn by a Sikh, one of the five Ks or external articles of faith that identify a Sikh (Kesh or uncut hair, Kara or steel bracelet, Kanga or a wooden comb, Kachera or cotton underwear, Kirpan or small steel sword).

[27] Someone who does not take action.

interviewer. I see she has kept her recorder aside, is sitting with her elbows on the table, too involved in my story to remember the formal reason for which she is here.

'What did you do?' she asks.

'What could I do? What does one do in such situations? Just stop thinking and do whatever you can lah!'

So, I finished my A-levels and told Papaji I would start working. Bhai already had a scholarship; we did not want him to give up his studies. It was easier for me to give it up.

'But what about the people in the band? Didn't they talk?'

'Of course, they did! They talked and talked, said Papaji should be ashamed, that he wanted to live off his daughter's salary. Only this time, Bebe was quiet. She didn't want me to work but also knew we needed the money.'

Every evening, I would watch Papaji sit quietly in the little sit-out outside our quarters. The rebab had long broken, his songs fallen silent. Then one evening, I made up my mind. I went out, sat next to him and told him about my decision, that I would start teaching in a school.

He'd looked at me as if I had lost my mind and said, 'But puttar, what will people say? What will they think of me?'

'I think at that moment *Wahe Guru*[28] provided me with the answer. I'd looked Papaji in the eyes and said, "Papaji, we know what is in our heart, *mere Guruji nu patha meri dil di baat*. What does it matter what people say?"'

The chickpeas have turned out exactly the way Bebe used to cook it. It stands in a simmering golden gravy of onions and tomato, fragrant with cloves and cardamom, piquant with the

---

[28] The wondrous teacher who dispels darkness and bestows knowledge.

use of *deggi mirch*[29]. I've cooked it over a slow fire, stirred and turned it till the chickpeas and spices, herbs and salts, oil and water are blended, and there is no telling one from the other, each fibre indistinct, immersed in a melting curry.

I quickly pack it into large *tingkat* containers[30]. I will drop it off on the way at the boys' home I have served for the last so many years. Before I leave, I give Miri and Piri their meal of fish and rice. I can hear the rustle of Baljit's newspapers outside the kitchen, his loud expectoration as he clears his throat. Four decades of marriage have taught me to read the signs, I know he is restless for his mid-morning cup of tea, but too embarrassed to ask in front of an outsider. My interviewer watches as I roll out the *rotiyan* for lunch, my fingers coated with flour, like nimble white mice.

'Soon after I got a job, my parents started a desperate search for a suitable boy for me. We were lucky, they found a boy quickly enough—Baljit had just returned from the UK, all he wanted was an educated girl . . . So, you see, my education came in handy after all!' My interviewer and I laugh together.

By the time I reach the gurdwara in Towner Road, the *ardas*[31] has already begun. I weave my way through the *sangat*[32], the rows and rows of white clad figures, their heads bowed.

---

[29] A blend of chillies for extra spiciness.

[30] Tiffin carriers.

[31] A prayer that is a part of prayer service at a gurdwara. It can be said at the end of congregational worship, after particular ceremonies like naming or cremation and/or as part of daily rituals. It consists of three parts: the first recites the virtues of the ten Gurus, from Guru Nanak to Guru Gobind Singh, the second recites the trials and triumphs of the Khalsa, and the third salutes the divine name.

[32] The congregation at a gurdwara.

Today is Bhai's sixty-eighth birthday, it has been forty-three years since I met him last. That tall, reed-thin body that no number of parathas fried in ghee from Bebe's kitchen could fill out, those large brown eyes that looked at the world with a kindly light.

The day I had met him last was the day of my wedding with Baljit.

That evening, for some reason, Bhai had been in a hurry to eat his dinner. By then we were quite used to his rather unpredictable manner, the way he would suddenly seem so restless. When he had sat down to eat, the wedding banquet was still not ready, the rice was still hard, undercooked. I could see his jaws masticate the food, moving up and down like pistons.

A high wind had gathered momentum as the evening progressed, a squall that howled outside our windows, playing havoc with the fairy lights Papaji had strung at our door.

I heard the clatter of the tin chair as Bhai pushed it back. It surprised me when he walked towards me and Baljit, put his arms around me. I had felt the knob of his shoulder, his thin back like a child's. His head had sunk into the hollow of my shoulder. Later, my arms felt strangely empty, the chill of the rain finally seeping into my bones.

'What are you doing, Bhai! Why are in such a hurry? Are you going somewhere?' I'd whispered urgently.

'Even if I feel I'm doing something wrong, *Wahe Guru* knows right *mere dil di baat*[33], he knows what's in my heart?'

---

[33] Guru Granth Sahib begins with the Japji Sahib composed by Guru Nanak, the 1st Guru of the Sikhs. In it, in the 6th *paudi* (section) appear the words '*Tirath nawan je tis bhawan win bhaney ki naey kari*—a mere dip in sacred tanks and rivers at a pilgrimage is no avail, divine grace can be obtained by leading an honest and truthful life. In fact, the Japji Sahib goes on to list down various paths—fasting, quietude, intellectual forays into spiritualism—but none are of

he'd asked, still clinging on to me, his body limp as if it would crumple if I pushed him away.

'Yes, yes, of course Wahe Guru knows,' I had answered a bit too quickly, not really stopping to understand what he asked, embarrassed by the many eyes that looked at us at that moment.

My eyes flutter open of their own volition. The *granthi*[34] is reading the very last lines of the ardas:

Those who dwelled on God's Name . . .
did not utter a sigh nor faltered in their faith
*   . . . remember their glorious deeds and utter O Khalsa*
Ji, Waheguru!

The familiar words wash over me—words that I utter almost every day of my life, words that I have heard Bhai utter so many times. They stop my fall through the green sludge, whirling sand, and the bits of root, and I don't know if I walk on land or on clouds. I feel the strength of the arms around me, a flash of warm sunlight on my face. After the long, hectic morning, finally, I know rest. I can go home and sleep for a while; I know there is no need to look through those letters now.

---

any avail without truth. Truth, as the gyanijis explain, is that which is in tune with the eternal law which controls the universe, and which is embedded in the very depths of the human soul. Guru Gobind Singh had said, 'He who has realized the Divine within is the true Khalsa.' Sikhs believe that in the normal evolution of things (as in slow cooking), as one follows the path of self-less service, meditation and honesty, one is automatically bestowed with the ability to discern between right and wrong, and this eventually leads to divine realization.
[34] The person who sits by the open *Guru Granth Sahib* reading the holy text at the gurdwara

BUDDHISM

Tamonata Sutta, *Anguttara Nikaya, 4:85*

bhikkhus, there are four kinds of people in this world . . . one who travels from darkness to darkness, one from darkness to light, one from light to darkness, and one from light to light

Buddhism

The Buddha, when asked who he was, did not reply he was a saint or a yogi, but merely that he was 'awake'. His answer became his title—Buddha, with the Sanskrit root *budh*, means 'to wake up' and 'to know'. And so, the Buddha became 'The Enlightened One'. What this prince of the Shakya clan woke up to was a state of *Nibbana* (in Pali, 'Nirvana' in Sanskrit), a state that some describe as nihilistic in its implications of complete cessation, the final extinction of a fire. But in truth, what it extinguishes are the unwholesome mental states of greed, hatred, and delusion. A follower of the path of *dhamma*[1] attains a peace and calmness of the mind, the bliss of Nibbana, and knows a freedom that is unfettered.

What distinguishes this path is its fierce clarity. With unwavering scientific precision, it describes a journey from *dukkha*, a deleterious state of human suffering, to a cessation thereof. And in this flowering of the human spirit, there is nothing more important than the human mind. There is immense responsibility and solitary work involved in attaining such awakening. Balance is the key, mindfulness is the path, and self-knowledge the purpose, for as the Buddha said not long before passing into eternity, 'Therefore, Ananda, be a lamp and refuge unto yourselves . . . seek no refuge elsewhere.'

Theravada Buddhist-Burmese

The Theravada Buddhist-Burmese community of Singapore forms a subset of the 200,000 strong Burmese and the much

---

[1] Dhamma in Pali, Dharma in Sanskrit, refers to the teachings of the Buddha, the Law.

larger Buddhist group, which incidentally is the majority religion of the country. Nesting within, with strong links to both, is this group of Theravada Buddhists, adding up to almost 80 per cent of the Burmese in Singapore. Like the Theravadins of Cambodia, Laos, Sri Lanka, or Thailand, the community takes pride in the Pāli canon, considered one of the most complete Buddhist canons to have survived in an Indic language, and endeavours to preserve the *dhamma* as recorded in these texts. If naysayers mention Mahayana Buddhism, which compared to the original Theravada Buddhism, stresses the work of compassion in the world and not solitary revelation as the goal of awakening, then Theravada practitioners opine differently. As one of the foremost Burmese teachers of Abhidhamma in Singapore explains, 'Compassion can help a people survive. But the purpose of a religious leader is not survival alone, he needs to help his followers find happiness, clarity of thinking.'

That said, the Buddha's vision of reality being 'empty' and devoid of permanence, permeates all of Buddhist philosophy, and for an establishment like the Singapore Buddhist Federation, voices from diverse Buddhist schools of thought— be it Mahayana, Theravada, or Vajrayana—shape its thinking. What the Theravadins bring to the table is an intimidating erudition in the field of Abhidhamma philosophy, drawn from the *Abhidhamma Piṭaka*, a part of the Pali canon recognized by Theravada Buddhists as the authoritative recension of the Buddha's teachings. Unlike the *Suttas*, this particular Piṭaka is considered a comprehensive vision of the totality of experienced reality, a meticulous schematization of the consciousness of the Buddha as the Enlightened One moved from one end of his teachings to the other: simply put, from suffering to the cessation of suffering. And since Myanmar is one of the countries of Southeast Asia where Abhidhamma studies are most assiduously followed, the advent of scholarly Burmese monks is eagerly anticipated in Singapore.[2] As one such teacher points out, 'Conducting Abhidhamma classes is not easy as it demands we fulfil our intellectual capacity to the fullest,' and as such, while most Theravada temples of Singapore restrict themselves to daily worship and prayers, it is only at organizations with a more academic intent, like the Palelai or Sri Lankaramaya Temples or the Mangala Vihara of Eunos, where such classes take place, catering to the Buddhist community at large.

Yet another field of highly sought-after specialization for the Burmese-Buddhists is Vipassana Meditation. Monks bring expertise from Myanmar where, at ballpark estimation, 80 per cent of the Buddhist population have undertaken at least a quick course in Vipassana, a form of meditation that remains inextricably linked to Abhidhamma[3]. It is not only an alliance of purpose when the practitioner seeks that single-pointed mind to discern the Conventional Truth from the Absolute Truth, but it is also the same wading into the stream of consciousness, to understand with objective clarity our conditioned existence. It is a dissolving of the frontiers of self and consciousness, a certain centring of self in a safe place of stillness within. As a practitioner from Singapore mentions, 'It has brought a collective maturity from individuals following the path,' a journey facilitated by Theravada monks who conduct small group teachings and meditation retreats. According to her, in this, the past two decades have been of particular significance, for whereas the oldest

---

[2] Abhidhamma studies started in 2012 when the Ministry of Religious Affairs, Myanmar allowed Abhidhamma Centres in Singapore. Today, the monks who teach Abhidhamma are permanently located in Singapore and the Abhidhamma Centres can hold Abhidhamma examinations as well.

[3] It is maintained that while Abhidhamma analyses the interdependence of body and mind theoretically, Vipassana does the same practically.

Burmese Buddhist Temple of Tai Gin Rod (previously at Kinta Road) dates as far back as 1875, it is only recently that Singapore has seen an increasing advent of Abhidhamma scholars.

So, how do women fare in this community where, unlike in Mahayana Buddhism, the Theravada pantheon does not extend to include female bodhisattvas? Whereas women interviewees describe the situation in Singapore to be different from Myanmar, a second-generation resident does mention that even today at her home, women's hta-mein or sarongs cannot be included in the same wash-load as her father's clothes. It is considered debilitating to a man's spirituality[4]. It is also true that the movement to reinstate the lineage of Theravada nuns or *bhikkhunīs* was met with outrage by the Buddhist Sangha of Myanmar under the rhetoric of potential ascetic chauvinism. Not fully ordained nuns, but it is the precept-nun-novitiates or *thilashins* who still populate the streets of Myanmar in their robes of pink or yellow, and much of Pāli literature assume an unchallenged inequality, or at most, different domains of power for the sexes.

But if one is willing to keep aside the debate on whether the Theravada society offers a liberal or patriarchal framework for women, what the community in Singapore does share with its homeland is the wonderful relationship of bonhomous camaraderie between monks and the laity. Like in Burma, it is the laity that supports the monastic order, and it is particularly the women who bring food, robes, and items of daily use to the monks as part of their merit making. In the beautiful ceremony of *Kathina* or robe-giving at the conclusion of the rainy months of

---

[4] The reference here is to a particular Burmese concept, *hpon*, meaning the spiritual potential or power of a person. Across Theravada Buddhist societies of Southeast Asia, it is a popular belief that since the Buddha was a male, it is only the male who can attain the highest level of spirituality. Consequently, the *hpon* of the man is considered precious, valued by men and women alike.

vassa[5], the monks assert their collective purity, and in response in giving the robe, the laity express their desire to honour religious achievement: the maroon monk's robe becomes a symbol of the path to Nibbana.

Thus, the Burmese-Buddhist community of Singapore thrives, a surprising mix of orthodoxy and urbanity with the highly cerebral, introspective Theravada belief at its heart. Among the myriad ways it dares to strike a different chord is the idea of *mettā*[6], which much as it emphasizes *dāna* or giving and *karuṇā* or compassion, does not forget the self. According to Theravadins, *mettā* is not true loving-kindness if it includes excessive self-sacrifice for the one who gives. As an interviewee said holding out an open palm as if sand sifts through her fingers, 'Let go, let go, let go, let others flow with their own *kamma*. You think of yours, see how liberating it is.' It is only your own kamma that remains your lifelong responsibility.

* * *

Nibbana

My 'mita of happiness' has skin like creamy parchment. Does she wear thanaka? Underneath there is a hint of a flush that tells me that she is excited to see me. Is it me or is that swelling tide her normal response to life?

We break the ice with her grimace. Last evening, she lost ten years of work from her hard drive, plus the technician damaged the backup.

'It's ok,' she says, 'It's not his fault.'

---

[5] The three-month rainy season retreat for Theravada Buddhists; Kathina is usually celebrated in monasteries during October

[6] Pronounced 'myitta' in Burmese, loving-kindness

No? Why not? I try to imagine my response to something similar.

Besides her day job, she is also an author, carries the best literary traditions of Myanmar within her—Ma Ma Lay, Daw Amar, Khin Myo Chit—journalists and writers who wielded their craft with unbending will. But they were also mothers, holding their child close to their heart in the hope that a prison wall would not separate them.

She speaks of growing up in Burma—never too far from the prison wall—her parents, her Saya or venerable teacher, moments of quiet happiness stolen in the shadows.

With her I travel her country. She becomes the 'eye' through which I see. The moonlight gliding off the pagoda walls, the water she pours from a silver bowl on the Buddha carved of black stone, the mettā that flows to others, but also to herself. And the way this drives her to lead a fulfilling life in the teeth of despairing odds, lends to authors like Daw Amar the will not to let themselves disintegrate. It is the self that ensures the sense of gliding in sunbeams is never really snuffed out, that the circle does not come undone.

A row of swans leaves the water—one by one sliding off the surface with their silver-tipped wings, into the dark sky, leaving behind a shattering of diamonds. A final flutter before the majestic climb up, with moonlight glistening on their backs, the swish of their wings into the silent night.

It is the suffocatingly hot last days of *Tawthalin*[7], when the fretful inhabitants of Upper Burma call the sun a prawn-killer and hope the weather will break soon.

My open palms tingle a little, just a little, like a powdery drizzle on a mountain fern. *Thami*[8], I cry. Her gaze sweeps over

---

[7] Typically August–September.
[8] Term of endearment for daughter/girl.

me. The eye, left to right, right to left. Relentless, disciplined
is its arc. Checking if the bed linen is wet, making a mental
note of the finishing talcum powder. I hear her first chanting
of the day,

> *Mama matapitu*
> *Acariya ca natimitta ca*
> *Avera hontu*[9]

I mutter in response, *thadu, thadu, thadu*[10].

The wire gives her voice an unfamiliar crackle. It sounds
guttural, as if coming from the depths of the earth, from that
edifice, Peninsula Plaza[11], where traffic swishes by on wet tarmac
and the spotlessly white theatre building next door stares you
down like a queen. And yet, you take a few steps, cross the magic
threshold, and you are lost in a world of betel leaves and rubies
from Mogok, *matpe*[12] fritters and *chin-lon*[13] balls tied with a bit

---

[9] Pali words of the Mettā Sutta containing the Buddha's thoughts on loving
kindness, chanted by Burmese-Buddhists every morning and also on spiritual
occasions. Here the words mean 'may my parents/teachers, relatives and friends
be free from enmity and danger.' Theravadins believe among the advantages
of the Mettā Sutta is it helps the person sleep and wake in comfort, live and
die in peace. He is protected by the devas and is dear to humans. His mind
concentrates easily and he dies without being confused in mind.

[10] A wonderful concept among Theravadins that ties the community
together is of merit sharing whenever a good deed or an act of good kamma is
performed. Once the act is complete, the performer of the act says 'ah-mya' or
'come and share my merit' and the person at the other end says 'thadu, thadu,
thadu', meaning 'well done'.

[11] Peninsula Plaza in North Bridge Road, Singapore, is the centre of all
Burmese activity in the city.

[12] Small round peas.

[13] A common street game in Myanmar played with balls made of rattan where
the ball is kept afloat by using every part of the body but the players' hands.

of pink taffeta. Little signposts in a migrant's life—comfortable yet quite irrelevant. Once inside, our footsteps would slow down, the knot of our *longyi*[14] loosening a bit.

Upstairs is thami's shop—the outer, rather large rectangular space with the inner anteroom, like a butterfly with its dark, mysterious chrysalis. Outside, in the open-faced showroom festooned with Myanmar sarongs and colourful ladies' handbags, thami mans the till, while inside in the quiet anteroom her husband sits on a large swivelling chair. It is here, among the computer screens and chequebooks and rubberstamps with imperious faces that say 'A/c payee only', that the eye is installed. The eye through which thami keeps a watch over me and her mother in Yinmarbin Township of Upper Burma.

In those early mornings, she would sleep as close to me as possible to keep away the winter's chill of Upper Burma. Shadowy figures swaddled in white cotton with knees and arms intertwined—me, thami, thami's May May, and her two sisters. The roof of this house was not made of corrugated iron sheets then as it is now. It was the old-fashioned *wagut*, bamboo slats woven like thatch. She would wake and gaze at the criss-cross pattern of the bamboo, count the little golden coins of light that danced on the walls as dawn broke. Through the chinks in the hardwood walls would drift in the fog from the slow-flowing Ayerwaddy, and she would curl in even closer.

The brass bell[15] is struck outside. I know my wife would have already cleaned out the shrine, placed on it fresh jasmine

---

[14] Burmese sarong.

[15] A brass gong, triangular shaped, is struck with a wooden hammer at the end of the morning devotions to call all sentient beings to come and share the merits of the good deed done. It is to be remembered that every prayer service is conducted not to seek the blessings of the Buddha but as an endeavour to tread the path towards nibbana.

and roses from the shrubs in our garden. Soon monks[16] will arrive outside our home, solemn, silent in their maroon robes, and my wife will spoon into their lacquer bowls steaming rice and boiled peas soaked in sesamum oil. And as they walk away, a barefoot file with downcast eyes, our day will begin.

'May May, why did you let him in?' Thami's loud voice disturbs me.

'Don't you know our Yinmarbin Township is no longer what it used to be! It's so dangerous nowadays! The police crawl the streets, they comb through every back lane and alleyway. If it was safe, wouldn't I be right there, sitting next to Phay Phay?'

The crackle is back, making her sound like a television commercial, metallic and phony. Oh yes, of course, the sound I heard was not of the brass bell. It was the man's chains as he dragged himself around. From the corner of my eye, I can catch a glimpse of our storeroom door, it looks gloomy inside, piled high as it is with *phas*[17] of different sizes, glass bottles and jars containing our *ngapi*[18] and mango pickle, pounded tamarind and soybean wafers for the year. I see him shift inside, the wound at his ankle is festering, it drips sticky yellow puss on his rubber slippers.

'I couldn't turn him away from the door, thami,' I hear my wife say quietly.

'But why now, May May? Isn't it better for Phay Phay to be calm now, quiet in his own thoughts[19]? Have you even asked Phay Phay if he wants him in the house?'

---

[16] The long-held practice of daily alms-giving to the monks, an act that is considered one of compassion on the part of the receiver and the giver.

[17] Boxes made of palm fronds.

[18] Fermented fish or shrimps.

[19] Since the last moments are believed to affect rebirth, Buddhists believe that the calmer and more prepared a person is, the better is his rebirth going to be.

I look around me. There is incense burning in the corner of my room, the long spirals of smoke disappearing into the early morning light. A vase of lotus flowers, white with pale pink-tipped petals[20].

'And he might be a common convict . . . How do we know what he's done on the streets? How many people he has killed?'

I see my wife sit silently before the eye. I smile to myself. My thami was always the fiery one, the one whose pigtails came undone, who objected the loudest at having her ears pierced[21]. Whatever she did, she did with a rare spirit, never accepting anything without question. I knew how dear such people were to the Buddha, and I would place my hands on her head and utter the last words of our Shakyamuni, hoping she would always walk the same path of earnestness[22].

But if my thami is strong, so is my wife, as tough as the *pyinkadoe*[23] of Burma. Now, she pauses for a moment and I hear her say firmly, 'I know what your Phay Phay would've said had

---

[20] It is with the view of making the last moments spiritual and peaceful that the Buddha's statue might be placed in the room of the sick and dying along with incense and flowers. It is also a reminder of the impermanence of life since a Theravadin does not believe in soul theory, but only in the rise and fall of phenomena. Thus, immediately after the death, consciousness ceases, a rebirth consciousness of the appropriate kind arises, and is established in the subsequent existence.

[21] Ear piercing is the ceremony that is held for girls, while shinpyu or the novitiation ceremony is held for boys under twenty when they join the monastic order for a short while. The ceremony has become a part of Buddhist rituals in memory of the the novitiation of Buddha's son, Rahula.

[22] In the Mahāparinibbāṇa Sutta from the Digha Nikaya, these are the last words of the Buddha: 'Behold now, bikhus, I exhort you: all compound things are subject to vanish, Strive with earnestness!' Thus, with the single word, earnestness, indicating the presence of mindfulness, the Buddha summarized all that he had advised in forty-five years.

[23] Burmese hardwood, timber

I asked and had he been able to answer, "that's his kamma and this is mine[24].""

It happens far quicker than we expect, and that makes us wonder how long this cat and mouse chase has continued before the man found his way to our door.

It is on the same morning while we have breakfast that the wail of a siren shatters the silence and my wife and I realize at the same moment that the police are here. I feel the slight tremor in her hand as she quickly feeds me another spoon of the rice porridge[25]. The loud yowl, like on Martyrs' Day[26] mornings, sets the crows squawking in the tamarind tree, its delicate frieze of leaves shudders against my window.

The siren has stopped. We hear the thud of approaching boots. Heavy Doc Martens coming up our stairs. One–two– three, yes, that is the end of the stairs. He would be walking in through the door, left open for the monks to arrive. My wife puts down the bowl of porridge with a clatter. There is a clanking of chains as our guest from last night pulls himself in, hobbles to the furthest corner of his cheerless room. I imagine him in the darkness, the air heavy with the spice from the dry chilli, mould from last winter. Plastic sheets rustle as my wife pulls the cover

---

[24] Theravadins believe that whatever happens to one is determined by past kamma and that happiness lasts as long as the force of past good kamma. Good kamma is any act motivated by good intentions and mettā, while bad kamma is any act motivated by the unwholesome mental states of greed, hatred and delusion. The concept of kamma is liberating because it makes one responsible for one's own actions and no one else's.

[25] Rice porridge with a bit of dried fish roasted over a charcoal fire is a favourite breakfast dish.

[26] Martyrs' Day held on 19th July is to commemorate the assassination of Aung San and seven other Burmese leaders that happened in 1947.

over the eye. Thami shunned to darkness, worried, waiting for us to return.

My wife hurriedly leaves the room, heading for our outer room. Yet the boots do not stop. They stride closer and closer.

I recognize him from his voice—Ko[27] Latt, one of my old students, never very attentive in class. While I would be reciting '*namo tassa bhagavato*[28]' before we started lessons, I would see him fiddle with the electronic watch his father had got him from China. Later when he came back to me for a referral, I had tried my best to dissuade him from joining the police force. 'You're like my own son, Ko Latt. Come join us, join the movement.' But he had merely stared back, he always had the most expressionless eyes, like the glassy eyes of a *belu*[29] on a pagoda wall.

He has obviously decided not to take his boots off. I hear him pacing around the outer room, making the old teak floor groan and complain. I wonder if he has remembered to do *shi-khoe*[30] to his *sayar gadaw*, his old teacher's wife.

'Come Ko Latt, please help yourself,' I hear my wife say amidst the clink of china. That would be the *la pet*[31], maybe with a tray of our Upper Burma cheroots.

'Inspector Latt, please.' His words are slurred, thick with betel juice. He loudly expectorates into the spittoon.

---

[27] Title preceding the name of a young male adult
[28] A common Buddhist chant meaning 'Homage to the Blessed One, the Consummate One, the Supremely Enlightened One'. Every time a lesson is started, homage is paid to the Buddha, the original and greatest of teachers.
[29] A common mythological being, an ogre
[30] Paying respect. Teachers hold a very special place in Burmese society in memory of the Buddha, the greatest of all teachers, and they are separately mentioned not only in the Mettā Sutta but in the Pali Paritta as well: a person knows he is blessed if he has good teachers.
[31] Tea leaf salad

That was after '88[32], in this country of ours of revolutions. I, like my friends, had decided to leave Number 4 Yinmarbin Township High School and teach privately. All those young minds that we could shape and awaken, it was an exciting time, taking us towards an exciting future. But then the Movement always claimed our best and brightest. I knew it would take my thami as well. I moved her away just in time, out of our country, out of our lives, before she was swallowed by the yawning mouth of the labyrinth, the Movement that had taken away our children from every household in the Township.

The whole house rattles on its shaky foundations as Ko Latt pulls out a chair, dragging it over the wooden floor.

'There are sixteen bodies lined up outside this Township. Sixteen—shot from such close range that their skulls are shattered.' There's a flatness to his voice, as if he is giving a daily update to his superior.

'His will be the seventeenth. They've been robbing villages, plundering households. On last count, material worth 75 million kyats have been stolen.'

Ah, the outskirts of the Township! That is where the Po Win Taung caves[33] are. On the banks of the churning waters of the Chindwin, by the wooded hills, crested with crowns of white pagodas. As one walks by, one sees the colonnaded stairways rising through the thick growth of neem trees, the tolling of the distant bell in the monastery.

When thami was small, I used to take her there. We would wake up early and go to the monastery. She would walk up the stairs, her little hand clasped in mine, and a cool breeze would

---

[32] Reference to the 1988 uprising by the Burmese people against the military government

[33] The name means Mountain of Solitary Meditation; it is a cave complex carved into a sandstone outcrop.

lift the tops of the tufted trees, calls of song birds float up from the carpet of emerald green. We would rest a while in the shaded walkways where yellow flags planted by earlier pilgrims fluttered and the water from the earthen pots was chilled and crystal clear as it slid down our throats.

I know thami's first memories of the monastery come wrapped in gold—little coins of chocolate in gold tinsel. The elderly monk would teach her to fold her palms like a lotus bud and recite,

In the Buddha I take refuge
In the Dhamma I take refuge
In the Sangha I take refuge

and afterwards place in her hand a single nugget of delight, reward for coming so early. In those days of proscription, chocolates were rare. As her tongue entered the sweetness, I would see a look of contentment settle on her young face, and I would know that the sense of shelter would stay with her forever, a safe sanctuary that no one can threaten.

Later, she would sweep the monastery compound with an air of self-importance. She knew she was building up her treasure trove of good kamma for her future life[34].

'They'll all die violent deaths,' I hear Ko Latt say in that raspy undertone, without raising his voice a notch. 'In the name of the Buddha I have vowed, these thugs will not hold our country to ransom, steal and rob at will.'

I hear a heavy metallic whirring in the outer room, as if someone has set into motion a metal ball on a wooden surface.

---

[34] A Burmese child is taught young that one is responsible for one's own kamma.

Is that a pistol that he twirls on our table? I try to imagine my wife standing in front of him, drawing herself to her full height, in her buttoned down *eingyi*[35] with a handkerchief tucked in her hand. I feel a trembling in my toes, my eyelids try to flicker open.

There is a shuffling movement from the storage room, rubber slippers stained with blood being dragged across the floor as quietly as possible. That ragged sound of breathing that I hear—is that mine or thami's from behind the eye?

'I joined the police force of this country because I'm a patriot, a *myo chit*. I'll serve my nation till the end, no force on earth can stop me.' Finally, there is a tremor of emotion in the voice, it shakes with self-righteousness.

But the Burmese pyinkadoe replies, as taciturn as she always is, 'Our country has known many *arzanis*[36], Ko Latt. Who is not a patriot here?'

At the beginning, the swans fly in formation, their shell-pink wings moving perfectly in unison. But as they climb higher, they gradually scatter. The moonlight takes them away, the drifting clouds, now silvery too, mesmerizes them. One of them looks down at the distant sea, the pin-pricks of light that rise and fall with the waves, and lets out a long forlorn screech.

I cry out, 'thamiii'. My limbs feel heavy, as if shackled down to this bed. The darkness weighs me down, a thick blanket that cuts off all light. I want to stretch out my hand, feel some warmth, hold her like I used to . . . the way I had held her that day when it rained and rained . . .

My daughters used to go to a school in the neighbouring township then, the best school in this part of our country.

---

[35] Buttoned blouse or shirt/jacket
[36] Person of courage, prepared to sacrifice his life for his convictions, martyr.

That day with incessant rain, the three sisters were caught in a stalled railway compartment. Hours passed, evening turned to night, and yet no help came; the train tracks remained immersed in water. When they reached home, I had held her close. My thami, my youngest. As I towelled her dry, I could hear the wild beating of her heart. That night my wife cooked a curry of roselle leaves and shrimps for them, fried in sesamum oil with bird-eye chili. It is a dish that thami cooks even today, whenever she misses home, a dish that we cannot bring ourselves to eat any more ever since she left.

I feel angry as I think of the fear I had felt in thami's heart that night, fluttering like an injured bird; resentment at the way the establishment always lets us down—why could not there be better schools nearer home, a better railway service, a better system that took better care of our children? I want to fling off the covers and let out a loud scream.

No, no, no, this will not do. I need to quieten down; I don't want to feel all that old anger. I say softly to myself, '*Maraṇaṃ, maraṇaṃ*, death, oh death, the pure, the exalted, the beautiful; my only constant companion[37].' I think of my feet, the soles— thickened and calloused with all the walking I have done all my

---

[37] The reference here is to Marantānussati or recollection of death which is a Vipassana kind of meditation when a person reflects on death and hence the impermanence of life. The contemplation starts with thoughts like death *will* take place, since no one is exempt. Such a practice is believed to create a sense of urgency and eventually helps in conquering attachments. As perception of impermanence grows, the person feels no fear, horror, or confusion at the time of death, and according to Visuddhimagga VIII:41, even if he does not attain nibbana in this life, he is at least headed for a happy destiny after death. The Buddha believed that rather than shunning all thoughts of death, it is rewarding to meditate on it as an existential reality. A Theravadin is constantly mindful of his attachments for attachments lead to afflictions and afflictions lead to bad kamma. As the Dukkha Sutta says, With the cessation of clinging, cessation of existence (bhava); with cessation of existence, cessation of birth (jhtāti).

life. The rich loam of our riverine land has entered into me and left a residue under my skin. My feet will soon die, for nobody is exempt. I think of my hands—with their deeply etched lines that once told me what my life would be like, whom I would love, whom I would hold in an embrace. Now I have passed it all by. My hands will soon die, for nobody is exempt.

As I say the words, my mind calms slowly, my breathing settles. Darkness holds no fear anymore, I enfold it, listen keenly to its voice, like that of a friend.

'Saya,' I hear it say.

'Saya, have you forgotten me? Its Aung Myint, Saya, I used to be your student at the Yinmarbin Township School.'

Unknown to me, the man had emerged from his hideout. He sits now on the floor by the foot of my bed. I can see his head, his long hair unkempt and matted that has not felt the snip of a scissor in months. I know a moment of panic. From the corner of my eye, I can see my wife has nodded off on the easy chair. The oil lamp that she had lit by the idol of the Buddha burns low, the smoke inky with soot.

'I'm not a common convict, Saya-gyi. You taught me, I used to come to this house in the evenings after school, *Sayar gadaw* would fry fresh fritters for us on rainy days.'

I can hear the smile in his voice at the memory.

But why have I not seen him in so long?

'After democracy came to our country, I left the Township, went back to my village in Pathein. I wanted to be close to the roots of my country, open a school, put to practice everything you taught me.'

I feel something old stir inside me—that sense of excitement and hope and apprehension, all tied up into a tight juggernaut that I used to feel every morning before I left for school. I strain to hear what he says.

'At first, it was perfect. We had our house on stilts, my wife would grow watercress and mustard greens in her little patch, I'd set eel traps in the river. I opened my school in our veranda and gradually, by ones and twos, it filled up with children. The mornings were alive with children's voices, you could hear my students learning their tables from a long distance away.'

I, too, remember that sound even now, sharp as the morning sun, dispelling all doubt.

'But then, my wife got pregnant and fear struck in my heart. The child was coming to us after a long wait of five years, and I knew in this village, where the clinic had closed down six months ago and only a midwife visited every other fortnight, my child wouldn't be safe. I tried to convince my wife, but she wouldn't listen. You know these women, Saya, always obstinate! She'd made friends, she said, in the village, they gathered to talk every evening when the men went out fishing . . .'

The man pauses for a moment, I can see in my mind the distant horizon, overcast with clouds, women sitting around on the terrace of a monastery, the older ones puffing on a cheroot.

'She was well into her third trimester when one night her water broke prematurely. The village women came to help, but by next morning, my child had started turning yellow. He had convulsions all night, Saya, rigours that just wouldn't stop . . .'

I hear my wife stir in the easy chair.

'That's why when the coup happened this year[38], there was nothing to hold me back. I went underground, hid in the jungle and joined an armed resistance group. I'm not a common criminal, Saya, we work to free our country[39]. . .'

---

[38] Coup of 2021.

[39] Working for one's country is considered good kamma as it is motivated by good intentions, and democracy, with its rhetoric of discipline and mindfulness, has acquired moral overtones.

I see those eels caught in a trap, they writhe and flail in the cane basket. My thami caught in the railway compartment as the waters rise around her.

'Why didn't you think of leaving the country, while you had the chance, like I did?' That is thami. The wires have woken, in their rustling I can feel her presence.

Her voice sounds unusually harsh, or is it just the distance, those interminable miles that separate us now forever?

'You could have got away, maybe worked hard and then you could provide your family with everything they needed, just like I do now!'

Thami, thami, thami, what are you saying! You were lucky, we found a good boy in Singapore, you set up shop after marriage, business swelled.

'But I didn't want to leave,' in the twinkling darkness I can see the man has now turned towards the eye. 'I wanted to stay back. There's at least hope here, in the killing and fighting and escaping the police. It's only the Movement that now gives us hope . . .'

It is only the Movement that has always given us hope, I add silently.

'But don't you see my father's condition? After all that Phay Phay has done all his life for others, it is finally time he looks at himself, finds his own peace. Didn't even the Buddha seek his own salvation first[40]?'

I hear my wife sit up on the easy chair. Does she nod in assent?

---

[40] For a Theravadin, building up his own kamma and ensuring a good rebirth is a person's greatest responsibility, and Abhidhamma teaches to temper mettā with upekkhā. Thus, when one gives in loving kindness, one also needs to temper it with equanimity. At that moment of compassion, one needs to remember his own limits, for mettā to others also includes compassion for oneself since the Buddha himself had first sought his own salvation before in maha karuṇā, great compassion, he pointed to others the route to happiness.

I walk with thami through the tall grass of the university campus, our emerald island, locked behind old iron gates; if you touch the rails the rust crumbles on your fingers[41]. There are stories here of protests and deaths, of pride and an intense loyalty that no outsider can understand. I watch her as she picks the *gangaw* flowers. Their fragrance will linger in her little palms for a long time.

I hear the flurry in my wife's footsteps. The flap-flap sound as she walks quickly in her slippers woven from fibres of the toddy palm. We have returned from our morning visit to the campus, thami knocks urgently on the door; she is hungry for breakfast.

I wait for her to run in, place the yellow flowers at the shrine and call out, 'May May you should've come with us.'

But no, it is the sound of the Doc Martens—heavy and threatening. And this time they do not stop outside. From where I lie, I can hear him breathing hard, see the heavy gold band on his hand, he obviously still has his old obsession for expensive watches.

'Why don't you leave my father alone, Inspector Latt?'

It is thami who takes charge. I was correct when I had sensed her presence around me today morning. I see Ko Latt turn to the eye in surprise. Yet, he recovers quickly, clearly a man not interested in anything but what he considers his call of duty.

'Why don't *you* give up that traitor you are hiding and we can leave your father alone to his nibbana[42]?' he repeats my daughter's words to jeer at her and me.

---

[41] Reference here is to the Yangon University which through the years have been at the centre of students' protest movements. Built on the banks of the Inya Lake, the campus is called the mya-kyun-tha or Emerald Island by the Burmese.

[42] Nibbana is associated with the human mind in a state of complete calm with no wavering of emotion, either positive or negative. The Abhidhamma speaks of the mature mind which is sorrowless (asoka), stainless (vimala),

'Which traitor do you speak of, Inspector? We have with us only my cousin, a monk from the Shwenandaw monastery[43].'

As she speaks, a monk emerges from the distant doorway. His maroon robes swish down to his ankles, touching the floor.

I look at him and, for some reason, cannot look away. Gone is the matted hair, the signs of the months spent in struggle and penury. Where is all the pent-up anger that I had heard in his voice last night? The morning light falls on his bare shoulder, lending a luminosity to his high, clear forehead. His calm eyes, like the petals of a rising lotus, gaze at the world with a new softness. Behind him, the long-winded whorl of incense smoke rises towards sublimity.

'My cousin was on his way back to the monastery, but then the rainy season retreat started, and he decided to join his brotherhood here in the Yinmarbin Township.'

I see by the storage room door offerings prepared for monks—yellow robes neatly rolled and placed in shiny black lacquer cups, each crowned with lotus flowers and the tall Lenten candles[44].

With difficulty, I bring my hands together like the bud of a flower, whisper, *thadu, thadu, thadu.*

A pale-yellow sunlight filters in through the open window of my room. It is tender with the promise of rain, the merciless dry spell of Upper Burma seems to be finally over. I try to turn to my side, I cannot hear their voices anymore.

---

secure (khema). The first step towards this is taking ownership of one's own kamma which makes vengeance pointless. Once nibbana is achieved, there is no rebirth.

[43] A beautiful monastery in Mandalay Hill, known for its fine teak carvings

[44] Typically for Kathina which is the largest alms-giving ceremony of the Buddhist year, occurring at the end of vassa or the monsoon months, though such lacquer cups are prepared for other occasions as well. The monsoon retreat is the time of the most intensive meditation for Buddhist monks.

TAOISM

Tao Te Ching, 47

the Master arrives without leaving, sees the light
without looking,
achieves without doing a thing

Taoism

Taoism is one of the oldest mystical traditions that has preserved in all its subtlety the original sense of human unity[1]. What it speaks about is the *Way of the Tao* or the way of final reality or authentic human life, that is, a life that is lived as close to the rhythm, creative force, and subtle dance of nature as possible. It is this that is the ordering principle behind all life for as Lao Tzu, the Master himself, mentions in the *Tao Te Ching*, there are only three things to teach—simplicity, patience, and compassion: simple in action and thought, you return to the source of being; patient with both friends and enemies, you accord with the way things are; and compassionate towards yourself, you reconcile with all beings in the world.

Taoists honour balance, above all the masculine yang energy. But with equal spontaneity, they embrace the sacred feminine, the valley spirit or the nourishing yin. For in this universe of constant transformation, it is in the ever-shifting patterns formed by the yin and the yang that the Sacred Tao finds expression. It is from the Tao that we are born, and it is in the Tao that we disappear. It is the great void, the fathomless non-being which effortlessly brings into being the myriad things, and into which all things must revert after fruition. Contemplating on the impartiality and all-encompassing nature of the Tao means setting one's vision beyond the conventional good and evil[2], beyond the necessary attachments and aversions. And the more detached one grows, the more passionately it teaches us to live. There is no stoical withdrawal from life here, but a

---

[1] Can you coax your mind from its wondering/and keep to the original oneness? Tao Te Ching, 10.

[2] What is a good man but a bad man's teacher/what is a bad man but a good man's job? Tao Te Ching, 27.

delightful immersion. So, the Taoist monk laughs uproariously, the cosmic gourd grows, lumpy and irregular, content in the knowledge that it holds the seeds of the Tao within, indifferent in its creative potential.

Chinese-Taoist

The Chinese-Taoist community of Singapore, though it straddles several dialect groups including Mandarin, Cantonese, Hokkien and Hainanese speakers, surprisingly makes up only around 8 per cent of the total population of the country. When asked, interviewees eagerly clarify that some followers of Taoism might not have a definitive sense of identity because of the syncretic boundaries with Buddhism and Confucianism that their faith has traditionally shared. It is true that elderly members of the community, as they rummage through their first memories of visiting a Taoist temple, do speak of a myriad colourful image— the temple ramparts of leaping dragons and rising phoenix, festival days when smoke would rise from the tall, pillar-like joss sticks, and the temple hall where Hindu gods and bodhisattvas jostled with Maju, the Sea Goddess, protector of the seafaring residents of Singapore.

Among other schools of Taoism, the community of Singapore primarily traces its lineage from both the Zhengyi (Way of Orthodox Unity) as well as the Quanzhen (Complete Perfection) movements. Pre-dating the Han and the Song dynasties respectively, this, if nothing else, establishes the antiquity of the faith. So, does such an old faith struggle to find followers among the young? The Taoist Federation, formed in 1990, or the Taoist Mission, formed in 1996, do speak of their youth outreach programmes and community demographics do seem skewed towards the elderly. As an interviewee—who is a young mother as well as an ordained abbess—confides, as a Taoist she was largely unaware of the practice of her religion. For the first years of her life, it was nothing but a tick in a box when submitting personal details. It was only when her father was on his deathbed, and she realized she knew nothing of her faith— neither in theory or praxis, that she could call upon to console her dying father that she actually took an interest in Taoism. Today, the Taoists of Singapore hold out a rich spectrum—it ranges from the Kew Ong Yah Temple of Upper Serangoon Road which was established as far back as in 1902 with incense brought in from the Temple of the Nine Emperor Gods of Penang; to single-room seminaries where young followers gather, away from the myriad gods of the Taoist pantheon to learn the skills of meditation. Somewhere in between comes an establishment like the Taoist Mission, housed in the beautiful Temple of the Jade Emperor[3] in Telok Ayer. On one hand, if it serves the community in its daily worship of resident deities, it also progressively works on awareness and identity building as it seeks to address the theological and soteriological needs of followers.

The latter brings to mind notions of salvation and the question, *what is the final objective of Taoism?* Is it to seek blessings of the Three Pellucid Ones[4] or to find guidance in the stars and constellations?

---

[3] The Jade Emperor in Taoism is one of the representations of the first god and an assistant to Yuanshi Tianzun, one of the Three Pure Ones.

[4] Three Pellucid Ones or Three Pure Ones form the Taoist Trinity, the highest in the Taoist pantheon. Yuanshi Tianzun is the Primeval Lord of Heaven and includes the energy of all the planets, stars and constellations as well as the energy of God; Lingbao Tianzun is the Heavenly Lord of Spiritual Treasures and includes the energy that exists on the surface of our planet and that sustains human life; Daode Tianzun who manifested himself in the form Lao Tzu, the founder of Taoism, includes all of the energies inside the planet as well as the five elemental forces.

An abbess and resident Master of a well-known temple answers, 'They are all important but eventually they, the Gods, the Immortals, the scriptures, the meditation, are all the means to an end.' And the end is to find oneself attuned to the Tao[5]. There is an implication of naturalness and spontaneity here; even a breath, a moment of thought can be a dividing wall. For, as they explain, a man of the Tao lives in the Tao, like a fish lives in water.[6] It is like the Chinese ideogram, where pictures represent the world with no intervening sign for a sound or name. And so, the man of the Tao enters the forest without moving a blade of grass.

How does this happen, this kind of seamless unity? At the core of Taoism is *wu-wei*—a philosophy of non-interference or non-action. Mistake this not for a moment to mean laziness or laissez-faire or mere passivity. It is a doctrine of intelligent submission to the natural order of things. To go with the grain rather than against the grain so that objectives are achieved with the least amount of energy spent. Thus, a pine branch cracks under the weight of the snow, but a willow merely springs back once summer returns. A tortoise enjoys dragging its tail in the mud, the painting paints itself. The point here is to get it intuitively, verbal comprehension is not enough, the Tao is a matter of inner vision.

The path to such vision lies in understanding the yin and yang. It takes us away from conventional morality—the covenants of good and bad, ugly and beautiful, value and worthlessness

---

[5] The Tao possesses enormous strength, the best image of the Tao being of water—most gentle, yet it overrides the hard; most weak, yet it nourishes everyone without striving.

[6] The water nourishes the fish, and the fish swims happily, not even conscious of the water. Take the fish out, and it struggles. Let it back in, and it glides smoothly, not leaving a ripple.

that society has taught us[7]. Instead, it is an explicit duality that merely expresses an inner unity: when everyone knows light, darkness is already created, when everyone applauds beauty, it exists only because of ugliness. The disappearance of one means the disappearance of the other. The existence of both makes for a wonderful wholeness, a celestial equality that emerges from these two energies which are of equal power and perpetually wrestle with each other for dominance. Thus, an artist's favourite vision of the yin and yang is of a crouching tiger and a flying dragon—both full of sound and fury. When they find balance, perfection is created.

It is because of this that classical Taoist worldview urges the embracing of the feminine—the receptivity, flexibility, passivity and silence that it embodies. Hence, Taoist cloisters offer women an alternative to family life and a common stereotype is of a wife and mother who becomes a recluse and renunciate, a religious leader and eventually 'Perfected'. Of course, feminists rightly point out that this does not necessarily challenge the patriarchal structure of the Chinese society. However, what it does do is bring to the forefront the importance of yin or the more feminine qualities. A Taoist knows that even as he progresses on his spiritual path, it is only at the beginning that the yang spirit of enthusiasm and inspiration comes in handy, for the final fruition he needs to cultivate the yin elements of commitment, discipline, and unification. The Master sits passive—the entrance into life occasions him no joy, the exit from it awakens no resistance. He knows life and death are parts of the same transformative process.

---

[7] When the great Tao is forgotten/goodness and piety appear/When the body's intelligence declines/cleverness and knowledge step forth/When there is no peace in the family/filial piety begins/When the country falls into chaos/patriotism is born. Tao Te Ching, 18.

Yet, despite an unwavering eye on the transcendental, the Taoist view of the self remains remarkably body-affirming. It is the human body that forms the microcosm of the universe, an alchemical crucible, a residence for divine presence, but perhaps, most importantly, a sacred space for the manifestation of the Tao. In a constantly transforming world, a Taoist likes to stay in touch with his ancestors[8] for it is through this lineage that he can connect back to the Tao. And as his soul touches the soul of the world, he sails rather than rows, glides rather than flies and finds himself dancing like Zorba.

* * *

Nothing At All

Why did the grand old lady of the temple, my 'mita of nothing at all', who should have appeared a stranger, feel the most familiar of them all? She did not have any of the Indian/Hindu connections I had clung on to earlier. The Jews, too, I knew well from my childhood in Calcutta; the Eurasians by their Christian roots from the Ave-Maria-inscribed walls of my missionary school; the Burmese were old friends from an earlier book. It was Taoism that was brand new. And yet from the moment I set foot in the temple, there was a sense of closure, of the different threads of culture that I hold inside me coming together, of a peaceful reconciliation with my past.

---

[8] The Tao predates the manifest universe, and will not cease to exist when this cosmic expression disappears, nor will it be diminished. The pantheon is not permanent, they are finite and ephemeral and will eventually become reabsorbed in the Tao's totality. As far as humans are concerned, the yang aspect of the person ascends heaven and becomes an ancestor for a finite number of generations.

Was it the antiquated structure of the temple? What was this feeling that I had of being thrust suddenly into the epicentre of life itself?

Mita or Minxia (name changed) rather nonchalantly explained to me the way of the Tao, with a shrug of a shoulder here and a passing instruction to a novitiate there. And by asking if we are conscious of the air we breathe, she took away without preamble the reins of the chariot I held in my hand. The reins that I hung on to in sheer desperation for fear of dear life. Instead, what she slipped into my grasp was the entire golden expanse of the sky.

I write her story in epistolary form, through a series of imaginary emails. Part of it is because I was reading the great Balzac's Mémoires de deux jeunes mariées *at the time. But more importantly, I needed to feel that with each letter, I was getting to know her a bit better, navigating another stair of the stepwell, such was my desperation to hold a cloud and pin it down.*

15 November 2020

Dear Mingxia,

Today morning, visiting the temple for the first time was quite an experience for me. Here I was, having packed off hubby and daughter to office and school respectively, sitting at my desk to write a quick, few lines—in fact I have been hurtling between a quick something or the other since I can remember. It was for a submission for which I had already missed the deadline, time was short, and the journey between beseech/appeal/request and quit/backoff/acquiesce was a harrowing one. It wore me out, I broke into a cold sweat edging through narrow spaces— the piles of books, pens which had run out of ink, a wilting chrysanthemum.

So, by the time I crossed the high threshold of the temple, I felt I had already run half a marathon. And yet that is where

Lao Tzu sits, his flowing beard the colour of the yellow clay which
had moulded the first man. In the hall in front were the gods
of the three realms, the Pellucid Ones, the Sixty Constellation
Protectors. Food was being offered at the high altar[9]—mounts
of mandarins in the twinkling gloom. It was an intensely strange
world—the soft, swaddling darkness, the heavy cinnamon-
scented smoke[10]; and yet why did it appear oddly familiar?

Beyond the temple was the open courtyard and it was here
that with the fiery unpredictability of a tropical storm the skies
opened up. Rain beat down on the delicately fluted temple
roof; a spate from the elegant swallow-tailed edges added to the
deluge. The overladen sky crowded in, lending to this universe
an overarching, thunderous cupola that spoke with the voice of
the first world.

I stood there for a while, caught in the cross-traffic of sound
and fury. Cymbals crashed in the temple behind. The cavernous
mouth of the Ancestral Hall lay ahead. I felt this is where I leave
all manifestations behind and walk into the mystery. It seemed
to wait for me, a throbbing, mystical presence. My heartbeat
quickened, I blinked once or twice, rubbing my eyes to see
through the rain.

And yet . . . there was nothing at all. As I dashed through
the rain and up the few stairs to the Ancestral Hall . . . there was
nothing at all. Just an empty room[11] with a few Chinese tea cups

---

[9] Both the human body and ritual altars are conceptualized as mountains
in Taoist virtual practice. A common Taoist phrase is 'enter the mountains'
(rushan) meaning 'to ascend the altar' for it is believed that the mountaintop
is the meeting point of man and God.

[10] Joss sticks are made from the trunk of a cinnamon tree. It is ground into
powder and mixed with sawdust and water.

[11] A void space is sacred in Taoism: We shape clay into a pot, but it is the
emptiness inside that holds whatever we want/We hammer wood for a house,

and a memorial plate for the thirty-six founding fathers of the temple. And some calligraphy like dancing grassland[12] . . . and apart from that . . . nothing at all.

Where was the tumbling, panting return to the origin that I had been promised?

A befuddled,
Nila

* * * * * *

My dear Nila,

Welcome to the temple-world. We use Lipton tea leaves by the way—nothing special at all. Did you notice the paintings of pine trees[13]? Oh, before I forget, did I tell you about the girl?

Abundant blessings of the Tao,
Mingxia

* * * * * *

Ah yes, Mingxia, yes, I did!

The gnarled pines of Chinese paintings that seemed to rise with a spatial lightness towards snow-covered peaks, down whose craggy contours flow tinkling mountain springs. Rise and fall, light and dark, they came to me with the music of an everlasting movement.

---

but is the inner space that makes it livable/We work with being, but non-being is what we use—Tao Te Ching, 11.

[12] Calligraphy is an important symbol in Taoism, signifying going with the flow of water, as if the brush writes by itself following the path of least resistance.

[13] Gnarled pines symbolize uselessness and so the impartiality of the Tao.

And underneath those walls you sat, with your hair pinned under a round master's hat. Do you know you remind me a bit of my aunt? Not the older one who was startlingly beautiful, married off to one of the richest landowners of Kolkata. Not the youngest one, either—dazzlingly intelligent, a bit mutinous as a result. You reminded me of the middle one—neither too good looking, nor erratic. With a loud, slightly harsh masculine voice that gave our conversations an unexpected boom, as if spoken by a professor in a coliseum.

PS: Which girl do you speak about?

* * * * * * *

Nila, what is the agenda? You call me your aunt and in the same breath you insult me—neither beautiful, nor intelligent—hanging uncertainly somewhere in the middle?!

Mingxia

* * * * * * *

No, no, no, my dear Mingxia. Uncertain? Most definitely not. Neither are you and nor was my aunt. Well-meaning? Yes. Comforting? Yes. But uncertain—most definitely not.

Plump and expansive, my aunt would sit on her divan with such ease that I felt, surely there was nothing on this earth worth worrying about. I would watch her go about her day, now pottering in the kitchen, now in her little vegetable patch, all the while looking as if she was in the deepest repose. Yet dishes would emerge from her fingers, cooked intuitively; pumpkins grew against a trellis as small as an armchair. As far as I knew, she had never ventured out of the bounds of her husband's home and yet seemed to possess a quick understanding of people. All my teenage friends in all their complexity seemed to disappear within her pillowy frame—the Gemini torn between boyfriends, yes, my aunt would nod implying the existence of past beaux; the Capricorn who could not let herself off the hook, my aunt would nod again indicating ambitions that she had foolishly allowed to get the better of her.

I do not know why I feel you share the same vibe—the restfulness, the repose. That was her, and this is you. The way your yin-yang robes are carelessly pulled on[14], the way your grey hair escapes in all directions from under your hat. You give the impression of someone who has never known the linearity of growing in a single direction. Instead, you hold diversity on a single rein, legends and stories surround you thick as leaves on a forest floor. Wispy bits of leaf and twigs raised by a storm seem to disappear in you without discrimination.

XXX in confusion and amazement,

Nila.

PS: Still no news on the girl BTW.

* * * * * * *

Dear Nila,

Do you know it is good to be silent? Once in a while to not respond to stimuli? It gives us time to clean our windows[15].

Do we see you again soon?

---

[14] A Taoist Master wears a white robe and over it a black robe to signify the balance of the yin and yang in the human body which in turn is a microcosm of the universe.

[15] Cleaning the windows is freeing the human mind from desire so light can filter in, the same light that helps one see the myriad things of the world outside. A Taoist believes desires act as a hindrance to both achieving inner

Forever in the all-encompassing Tao,

Mingxia

PS: Oh, that is Suyin, the new guest at our temple.

* * * * * * *

12 December 2020

My dear Mingxia,

You know it has been nearly a month since I've been going to the temple. Now and then, whenever time allows, I come, watch you turn the pages of your scripture with what looks like tarrow sticks[16], bask in the calm of the Master as he sits twirling his long, stringy beard[17], his eyes twinkling with Lord knows what half-forgotten joke. Some of the initial novelty has passed, and as I watch the white robes flutter on the clothes line, sometimes I cannot help but let my mind wander—my old ancestral home on the outskirts of Kolkata where the maids would bring the washing in from the terrace when it rained and hang them up inside. The rows and rows of billowing white cotton, if you sat under them, you could smell the starch, the snuggly smells of mothers and aunts.

But today, when you spoke about the yin and yang—how the thin line between them shows there is no perfection in this world, that the only perfection is when the two come together— somehow, I felt a wild surge of pleasure. As if somebody had suddenly unshackled me, as if all my old worries and doubts had

---

peace and outer freedom. Free from desire, you realize the mystery/Caught in desire, you see only the manifestations—Tao Te Ching, 1.

[16] Sticks made of bamboo.

[17] A Taoist does not cut his beard or hair since it is a symbol of continuity and connection with ancestors.

fallen away. I walked out into the sunshine. Beautiful harmony waited outside on the street where a dargah jostles with an Anglo-Chinese church, where everything comes together—the past with the present, the shore with the sea, the adventurous wayfarer with careful city commerce—and the rhythm of a dance burbled up inside. I wanted to rush in, touch everything, like a touchstone of truth. Everything, everything, everything, I muttered, in a moment of wild hope.

I feel drawn in, as if I was a part of this. As if finally, I am journeying from the gnarled pines and mandarin oranges towards an inner space—dark or lighted up, it does not matter.

See you soon.

An ecstatic traveller,

Nila

* * * * * * *

Hi Nila,

I am glad you experienced such joy. Well, the Tao affects different people in different ways. Sometimes, they ride the water buffalo to cross the garrison pass[18], disappear like the Iroquois woodsman into the unknown. Sometimes, they dance like Zorba, as you wanted to do. Sometimes they write odes to the virtues of wine[19]. They grow amused, uninhibited, watch the world go by indulgent as a grandma[20].

---

[18] Reference to Lao Tzu who, after realization, rode the water buffalo into wilderness.

[19] Reference to poet Liu Ling who wrote 'In Praise of the Virtues of Wine'.

[20] If you do not realize the source/you stumble in confusion and sorrow/When you realize where you come from/you naturally become tolerant/disinterested, amused/kind-hearted as a grandmother/dignified as a king. (*Tao Te Ching*, 16).

Enjoy the light of the Tao,
Mingxia

* * * * * * *

But Mingxia, what disturbs me is how little I know about you.
I am still a stranger to who you are as a person. Apart from
my first intuitions when I had bracketed you off with my aunt
(maybe, as is usual, it was my hasty judgement, but I know now
there is space for that as well in the great void of the Tao), I
know nothing. I draw a blank. Is it intentional?

And how about Suyin, have we not completely forgotten her?

* * * * * * *

My dear, you know nothing because there is nothing to tell. If you
take away the great big void, there is nothing. Nothing at all[21].

Like the many other Chinese of this country, my
grandparents came from the Hainan Island. Like a million other
girls, I went to Haig Girls' School, then college, then married.

Ours was a very normal Chinese household. We stayed with
our grandparents, our *zǔfùmǔ*, fought and laughed, ate and
sulked in turn. Every year we would celebrate CNY—the lunar–
solar festival when it is said yin completes its dominance and
gives way to yang. The celebrations would be the usual round
of *hong bao*[22] and firecrackers, eating *niangao*[23] till we groaned

---

[21] Mystical union with the Tao is the goal and as such, to be a separate
individual, especially one rooted in egoistic desires, is to be separated from the
Tao and so is not encouraged.

[22] Red envelopes for monetary gifts.

[23] CNY rice cake.

with tummy ache, and the red and gold *fu*[24] calligraphy on the doorway.

I am afraid there is nothing spectacular that sets us apart. Like you said, I am that not-very-sparkly middle aunt. 😊

Rest in the simplicity of the Tao,
Mingxia

* * * * * * *

Are you sure, Mingxia? There was not anything spectacular at all? I have myself known the purifying bath of childhood—it is magical, the light by which even a piece of thin cotton appears like an embrace of love. Did your childhood, too, not give you the feeling of living in places unlike any other in the world?

* * * * * * *

Well, if you put it that way, maybe then I should mention something.

It is true that after the kitchen god's effigy had been burnt, and the celebration of CNY was over, there would be no residue at all. We would go back to school and the girls would groan that another term had started, exams would soon be around the corner.

But it is also true that there were these little things I would notice afterwards. With the opening of the sealed doors and the sweeping in of good fortune[25], there would be a new cheer and purpose in our home. As the summer breeze would get warmer,

---

[24] For prosperity.
[25] The doors of a home, kept sealed, are opened on CNY morning to let in good fortune.

father would call out '*Zài jiàn*[26]' a bit louder to my mother when he left for work, get a bit more annoyed when *zŭmŭ*[27] reminisced about the great fog of Hainan, in the coastal town where she grew up, where it would creep in unannounced, seep into the walls and floor tiles, like a wet blanket.

It was almost as if in the months following CNY, I could see the yin-yang balance shift. And these little signs would, as you say, draw me in, make me feel a part of the great flow of energies. I hope that explains things.

In union with the Tao,
Mingxia

* * * * * * *

But Mingxia, my dear friend, do you not feel that the signs that you speak of were a part of the change of season? The very normal annual cycle? Does summer ordinarily not make us a bit more brisk, less tolerant of emotional indulgences?

N

* * * * * * *

Hmm, that is exactly what I said in the beginning, Nila. We are ordinary. If you take away these signs, often not obvious to the external eye[28], then there is nothing at all. Nothing.

M

* * * * * * *

---

[26] Goodbye

[27] Grandmother

[28] As original Taoist philosophy states, understanding it is a matter of the internal eye, of intuition rather than conscious thought.

13 December 2020

Dear Mingxia,

I write to you today after having spent a virtually sleepless night. I could not help but think of what you said about the internal eye, about the flow of energies, things that were not really visible to physical sight.

You know, in my ancestral home (yes, I insist on telling my stories) on the outskirts of Kolkata, it was rumoured a pair of snakes lived in my grandfather's room, the lucky charm of the householders. Every night, milk was left for them in shiny brass pots, and every morning the pots would be empty. Sometime in the night, while we slept, they had come, a pair of silent, slithering shadows and drained the milk. I would lie awake to see them, watch as the rising moon played hide and seek with the dark, and a soft-footed night descended. Yet every time they caught me unawares—I would wake to a bustling, sunny house and, yes, to the empty brass pots!

It was these two snakes—wise creatures of the ancient underground who came to us in darkness bearing good fortune for our home; who first woke me to the existence of a parallel world—a world that was unseen and could only be intuitively felt, and yet it moved with our every joy and sorrow. It rejoiced when a child was born, left the milk untouched when we grieved for the passing away of a brother.

So, my dear friend, when you speak of the Tao and invisible energies, was there a specific moment when you woke up to it? When it came and hit you, like the first realization of love?

An avidly curious,

Nila

* * * * * *

Dear Nila,

This is quite surprising. Had you come to the temple today, this is exactly what I would have spoken about—the magic of the inner eye.

It was in my early life, just after I had finished college that I dashed my family's dreams and became a florist. I set up shop in Ang Mo Kio, was trained by a German Master Florist. You know, earlier it was as if the flowers that had taught me the true meaning of rigidity—the way we would stick them up in those bits of sponge, on display like decorated generals. But under the German Master I learnt to flow with nature—the sweep of the foliage, the pared-down simplicity of green lichen on a river stone, miniature water gardens with light filtering through, casting gentle, dappled shadows on the walls. While working with my fingers, I felt the grace, the balance. In the tremor of the filaments was the trembling of the veil, at my fingertips were mysteries too big to fit into my little flower shop.

The shutters of the shop soon came down, I crossed the high threshold of the temple where Lao Tzu sits. I had to understand what seemed to lie just outside my understanding.

What happened afterwards? That is, I think, another story for another day 😊

In the yin and yang of life,

Mingxia

PS: In my next letter, I promise to write about Suyin. Please remind me.

* * * * * * *

Mingxia, do I need to beg for you to tell me? Do you not know how keen I am as I cross the same high threshold where Lao Tzu sits?

PS: Reminder—Suyin!

* * * * * * *

Nila, it can harm neither of us to beg a little, the Tao does teach us humility. But well . . . if you insist (which BTW, seems to be quite a habit with you).

So, I entered the temple. By then I was married with grown-up children, and to be fair, the first few years I worked really, really hard.[29] Under the ever-quizzical eye of the Master, I learned to read the scriptures, say them in all the dialects[30] that our followers required, laid out the food at the altar every morning, organized feast days[31] through the year. And as I got better at it, discipline, a virtue for any disciple, seemed to wrap itself around my neck like one of your snakes. I worshipped the Gods and served the congregation diligently, and yet, your snakes and my flowers continued to elude me. Days turned to months, and months to years, yet I struggled to walk those few steps from the outer hall to the inner sanctum. The more I tried, the further it seemed to get[32] and I realized rigidity[33] is a strange thing—it holds down the most well-meaning of us.

---

[29] Duties of an abbess include managing the temple, community service, spiritual consultation and promoting the Taoist identity.

[30] Taoist scriptures are written in Chinese but are read and pronounced in all dialects: Mandarin, Cantonese, Hokkien and Hainanese.

[31] Most important ones are for the Jade Emperor (ninth day of first lunar month) and for the Supreme Patriarch Lao Tzu or Laozi (fifteenth day of second lunar month).

[32] For aligning oneself to the Tao, one needs to go with the flow, give up trying to control it intellectually: The Tao that can be told/is not the eternal Tao. (*Tao Te Ching*, 1).

[33] To go with the flow, it is important to be flexible: Can you let your body become/supple as a new born child's? (*Tao Te Ching*, 10).

But then, one day, just after the autumn equinox, Suyin arrived at our temple. Suyin—a beautiful young girl with delicate features, a vulnerability that masked a strength that perhaps even she herself was unaware of. She had lost her eyesight in a car accident, the same unfortunate accident that had claimed the life of her fiancé and left her with burns and fractures that would take a lifetime to heal. The Master told her she did not have to do anything at all,[34] just surrender herself to the sun and the wind, told her that there was no better therapist than nature.[35]

And so, Suyin started living in the temple, and I took to watching her through the day, with the same keenness with which I performed my other duties.

I would watch her as she moved with the sun. She would wait patiently at the bottom of the three-storey pagoda for the sun to turn. As it did, she would get up with difficulty, and despite the pain, drag her chair to the walled garden at the back. There she would again sit, basking in the evening sun. It was almost as if she knew the path of the sun intuitively, as if she was tied to it in a bond as invisible as the one that tied the snakes to your ancestral home. Little things excited her—a powdery rain that she could lick off her nose with her tongue, a rustling in the bamboo grove that told her that the evening breeze had started, the long afternoon was over. I would watch her as she smiled to herself at these little miracles of nature,

---

[34] The reference is to wu-wei, the philosophy of non-interference: Do you have the patience to wait/till your mud settles and the water is clear/Can you remain unmoving/Till the right action arises by itself? (*Tao Te Ching*, 15).

[35] When one aligns oneself with the Tao, one flows with cosmic power and as such the power and force of nature is embodied within.

and over her head the Master would catch my eye in silent knowing, nodding at her virtues.[1]

And thus, my dear Nila, my story ends.

May we continue to live in the Tao,

Mingxia

* * * * * * *

But Mingxia, no, do not stop just yet. What happens after this? Were you able to move from discipline to a final unity? From the altar to the void?

* * * * * * *

After this? Hmmm, well, let us say that nothing happens, nothing at all. We repose in the great void, like your aunt reposed on her divan and watch as leaves and twigs, wispy butterfly wings disappear into its yawning depths; as it swallows without discrimination mandarin oranges and tarrow sticks, snakes and flowers, the yin and the yang. And we merely wait for the marathon to stop, and wonder if it should be beseech/appeal/request or quit/backoff/acquiesce.

---

[1] Reference here is to the Taoist concept of Te i.e., virtue or morality. From a Taoist perspective, Te is not moral rectitude or conforming to a set of received social norms. In fact, Te may be distorted through education and social systems. Rather, it is the way in which the Tao manifests as embodied activity, and in such manifestation, each individual is different. However, in speaking of some of the recognizable patters of Te, an interviewee spoke of the three central qualities of Taoism—simplicity, patience and compassion. From these all else flows naturally. Open yourself to the Tao/then trust your natural responses/and everything will fall into place. (*Tao Te Ching*, 23).

Does that give you an answer?
Yours forever in the void,[2]
Mingxia

* * * * * * *

---

[2] The Tao is like a well/used but never used up/it is like the eternal void/filled with infinite possibilities/it is hidden but always present/I do not know who gave birth to it/it is older than God. (*Tao Te Ching*, 4).
The Tao is like a bellows/it is empty yet infinitely capable/the more you use it, the more it produces/the more you talk of it/the less you understand. (*Tao Te Ching*, 5).

ZOROASTRIANISM

Gathas, *Yasna, 43.9*

when the Good Mind came to me and asked
what wouldst thou choose
before Thy Fire in veneration, I replied
So far as it is in my power, I shall cherish the gift of
Righteousness

Zoroastrianism

It was Zarathustra who emancipated religion from the realm of right and wrong and offered it to the universal man. Divinity dawned on this gentle prophet of Iran, and like Confucius, he travelled from province to province seeking a prince who would accept the white light of simplicity that his message held—that religion is a moral service to be rendered in love. In so doing, he never hovered out of the human horizon and neither did he speak of a single, indistinct grasp on the totality of the universe. Instead, it was a coherent, articulate pattern: that the world is a theatre of conflict between two diametrically opposed moral spirits and that the two worlds are defined in relation to the pivotal concept of *Asha* i.e., truth or righteousness. It is the *Vahu Mano* or Good Mind that enables one to grasp *Asha* and realize how every human state deviates from its ideal state of perfection. This, in turn, gives rise to Good Thoughts, which inspires Good Deeds, and which when articulated forms Good Words—the three basic tenets of the faith.

There is a clear existential duality here—light and the absence of light. It is their opposition in the perceived world that foreshadows human choice, and it is this choice—which every man must make for himself—that makes necessary the coincidence of intelligence with goodness. For it is the human mind that chooses wisely and so renews every moment the natural order of beneficence to all.

Thus, the seed of a sustaining world order lies in that single entity—the human mind. With the zest of a warrior, it picks the right side of battle, the right weapons, and protects the world from attacks of evil, and in so doing is a collaborator with God Himself,

Clear is this all, to the man of wisdom
as to the one who thinks with care:
He who upholds Truth with all the might of his power,
He who upholds Truth the utmost in his word and deed,
He, indeed, is thy most valued helper, O Mazda Ahura![3]

It is a path of freedom for man—freedom to exercise choice which is dictated by no external moral code but is adapted to every individual situation; freedom from fear for worship does not warranty boons but a purification of the mind; freedom to take ownership of simplicity as a physiognomy of perfection. It is a final release of the human spirit as it blossoms in the divine luminosity of Truth alone.

Parsis

The Parsis of Singapore is a tiny community which numbered a mere forty in 1974 and today stands at a still modest 350. The community remains small not only in Singapore, but even in India, their first port of call, where centuries ago they landed from the Persian Gulf, armed with their scriptures and holy fire. When asked about this, Parsis, inherently zealous raconteurs, love to narrate the story of 'Milk and Sugar'. That, more than a thousand years ago, alarmed by the influx of foreigners, when a local Indian king had shown them a silver bowl brimming over with milk, the Zoroastrian elders had sprinkled a spoonful of sugar in it, saying, 'The milk has not overflowed but has been sweetened.' And so, the sagacity of the elders had won the day, and the Parsis had remained, though, within their boundaries, not encouraging inter-community marriages and adapting

---

[3] Gathas, *Yasna*, 31.22.

some Indian customs, but most definitely adding a distinctive sweetness to the multiplicity of India. The idea of Parsi Baugs or Parsi Colonies comes from here, and fortunately a few of these little walled kingdoms have survived in Mumbai, bravely withstanding the rush of urbanization. A community elder in Singapore, while speaking of his childhood in India, recounts, 'We were kings out there, within the colony where everyone was Zoroastrian and wore a *sudreh* and *kushti*[4].' Though perhaps a note of caution is needed here—the Baugs of Mumbai are no Shangri-las of peace. They bustle with life and family gossip, and the haranguing by a bossy Parsi mum can often be heard from miles away!

As in India, in Singapore too, the Parsis grow deep roots, going far back to the 1820s when records show a Ruttonjie and Muncherjie being allotted land at Kampong Glam by Colonel Farquhar, Raffles' original city planner. There is mention of another Muncherjee as well. Like other Parsi traders of the time subjected to the turning wheel of fortune, he had his estates in Bencoolen sealed off when the British ceded to the Dutch. Unable to pay the mortgage, Muncherjee—a rich ship-owner and a 'fine-looking man' with the 'eyes of a tiger'[5]— was sentenced to work for life in chains and to him belongs the dubious fame of being the first Parsi convict of Singapore. With his name is also tied the history of Parsi Road of Shenton Way. It was when Muncherjee fell seriously ill that Parsi traders

---

[4] Sudreh means the Beneficial Path and is an undergarment made of thin white garment that Zoroastrians wear irrespective of gender to remind them not to stray from the right path. Kusti means 'the pathfinder' and is a girdle made of seventy-two strands of sheep wool, corresponding to the seventy-two parts in the Yasna recitation.

[5] The quotes are from descriptions provided by Frank Marryat, a midshipman who visited the Singapore jail at this time.

from China bought a burial place for Zoroastrians in Singapore. Later, though the grounds were cleared and the adjacent Parsi Lodge demolished to make way for urban development, the name Parsi Road remained, marking the site of the original cemetery, making Muncherjee a permanent part of Singapore's topography.

A Parsi's love for a good story is well known, interviewees speak of impromptu dramatic performances at home, with hastily rigged up props and table lamps improvising as flood lights. Consequently, it is perhaps not surprising that one of the most interesting Parsi legacies lies in the field of the performing arts. It was the Parsis who brought the *wayang Parsi* or Parsi drama to the shores of Malaya, and though they started with the ancient myths of India and legends of Persia, the audience was multicultural, and it was not long before these itinerant theatre companies started hiring locally to save money. This triggered the use of Malay, along with Urdu and Hindi, and before long *wayang Parsi* had taken root in Malaya and become the popular *bangsawan* of today. In Singapore, Khurshedji M Balliwala remains a legendary name: his Victoria Parsee Theatre Company played to full houses at the Novelty Theatre of Queen Street, and his plays like the *Inder Sabha*, a romance of a prince and a fairy with its special effects and flying *peris* (fairies) was what dreams were made of.

There are other Parsi names too—stalwarts who have left important legacies in Singapore[6]. Thus, Basrai ran the first public cinema in a tent pitched at the junction of Hill Street and River Valley. More recently, there have been notable names like Dr Jimmy Daruwalla, known for his pioneering work with

---

[6] The book *The Parsis of Singapore* by Kanga and Khaneja is an invaluable resource on the subject.

the Dyslexia Association of Singapore; Dr Dadi Balsara, the 'Perfume King of Asia' who launched the winning Singapore Girl Perfume; Mrs Nargis Medora who devoted her life to the cause of leprosy in Singapore. These pioneers in diverse fields—what made them such avant-garde thinkers, individualists driven by their own passions?

When asked, an interviewee, who is an ordained priest himself and yet has refused all his life to perform prayers for money, points to their faith, Zoroastrianism—one of the earliest revealed religions which is surprisingly modern in its focus on individuals carving their own customized paths towards perfection. The scriptures mention *Fravashi,* the divine spark that resides in all of creation, the means by which God's hand is present in every particle, and because of which God does not need to intervene from time to time in the evolution of creation. The Fravashi gives a person an intuitive access to the moral and ethical laws of Asha, helps him gain insight into the true nature of creation through introspection, endows him with natural talents that can be harnessed and developed through choice to achieve a higher calling. Thus, when a Zoroastrian enters an agiary, at its entrance is the *Farohar*[7], the principal symbol of the faith, a winged image of the Fravashi or personal spirit that lies within. It is what guides the Good Mind to lead the life of an Ashavan, i.e., a life of beneficent goodness to all,

With these hymns shall I come to Thee, O Lord!

To Thy Truth, aided by the deeds of the Good Mind,

Seeking earnestly the reward of the beneficent, and receiving it,

---

[7] Interpretations of the Farohar varies. It was first used as a symbol by a Persian Achaemenian King as a personal symbol of his kingship with grace or his Fravashi. In Singapore a Farohar adorns the entrance to the Zoroastrian House.

I shall be master of my own destiny.[8]

So, how do women fare in this community of migrant traders, under the umbrella of a religion that visualizes the ideal Zoroastrian as a soldier, armed with the sword of a Righteous Mind? While interviewees do speak of homes run by the iron-hand of a dominant mother, part of the answer goes back to the old 'Milk and Sugar' story. The restrictions placed on intermingling have persisted, and intermarriage is looked upon with skepticism by Parsis. Thus, inheritance laws remain unfair for women who marry outside the community, though after the Supreme Court of India's verdict in 2017, a Parsi woman married to a non-Parsi is now allowed to enter the agiary.[9] Interviewees, when asked about the fire temple that still remains out of bounds for outsiders, do speak of Iran where access is more open, and where Zoroastrian women can become ordained priests.

In Singapore, Indian traditions have persisted and the prayer hall of the Zoroastrian House[10] at Desker Road is yet to know a female priest. But times are changing. Who knows the future? And it cannot be denied that when Zarathustra uttered the words that form the last Ha of the *Gathas*,[11] he was advising his youngest daughter

---

[8] Gathas, *Yasna*, 50.9.

[9] A point to remember is all Parsis are Zoroastrians, but not all Zoroastrians are Parsis. A Parsi is a descendent of Persian ancestors who arrived in India from Persia, and one who has been formally admitted into the Zoroastrian faith.

[10] The Zoroastrian House is the only community hall for Parsis in Singapore and serves as the office of the Parsi Zoroastrian Association of Southeast Asia. There is no fire temple here, instead the prayer hall of the Zoroastrian House is used for prayers on Sundays and other auspicious days.

[11] The Gathas are the hymns composed by Zarathustra, with verses composed in the metrical forms of ancient Indo-Iranian religious poetry. In extent, the Gathas

at her wedding to make her choice with the counsel of enlightened understanding and he did address followers of both genders,

O ye, men and women!
When faithful zeal inspires your life,
When tainted thoughts and intentions are rooted out,
When the evil within you is destroyed forever,
Then shall the Blessed Reward be yours for the Good Work.
And if you fail, 'Alas, alas' shall be your final words![12]

* * *

Freedom at Last!

Mithra[13], *my 'mita of the confluences' has made her home at the convergence of worlds where paths fork, realms meet, where resides choice. She started by speaking about a mountain cemetery, in the shade of deodar trees, with few graves, where the worlds of life and death closely mingle. And led me to the end, where the sky dips low, the bole of a tree gives off a gentle fragrance, a golden sun hangs just below the horizon. She took me by the hand and together we took giant strides crossing over from the world of darkness to the world of light. She showed me it was possible, that we were free to decide. Yet, at the end of our journey, we found ourselves at the beginning of another, and there we sat on the banks of a bubbling river and spoke of surrender . . . yet again.*

---

constitute a small book containing about 6,000 words, in about 1,300 lines set in 238 verses which are collected in seventeen chapters, each called a Ha.

[12] Gathas, *Yasna*, 53.7.

[13] A Zoroastrian angelic divinity of light and contracts, the protector of cattle and of the waters, also one of the judges at the Chinvat Bridge that separates the world of the living from the world of the dead.

Have you ever had the experience of someone calling out to you
'You've got such Persian eyes' and you looking up, setting aside
the first flush of pleasure, to stare into a pair of Persian eyes
yourself? Well, that is what happened to me. Almost as if the
image that her words evoked, of a pair of dark hazel eyes with
eyelashes as deeply shadowed as the cypress gardens of Shiraz,
had by some means spilt out onto a canvas in front of me. As if
by a quirk of technology, my mind had found an extrapolation
into void, and the café where we sat by that conduit of commerce
called Cluny Road had transformed to a house of mirrors where
reflections bounced off each other into infinitude. What she
saw in me, I saw in her and with each image the understanding
deepened, carrying us down eons to shores of distant time.
It was as Tulli had maintained, 'There remains the homogeneity
of the stone to contend with.' Bricklayers build cities with grates
and gutters and of beauty that serve no practical purpose, yet
once we enter the stone, the unity of substance prevails.

I do not know if you have ever had this kind of an experience,
that feeling on a first meeting that you have known someone for
years, that you did not really need to ask any questions because
you already knew all the answers.

That morning though, that rush of sudden familiarity
unsettled me and it did not help that she stared at me with the
frank, open gaze of a child, and to top it all, yawned—quite
widely—within the first few seconds of meeting. Did she feel
she knew all the answers too? No, I do not know. Maybe I
will ask her one day—sometime later, during one of our long
conversations when we speak intermittently and sit for hours
in silence.

That first morning, that first yawn had me miffed. It had
not been easy you know, finding her—a sweaty walk in circles
around that garden where Singaporeans come for a breather,

and a serpentine canal winds its way through Lalang grass. The cuffs of my jeans were heavy with brushwood, my eyes with the steaming sun. Finally, I had grown tired of the search and called her.

'Mithra, where are you? Why can't I find you anywhere?'

'Look inside,' she had said. 'Why do you keep looking outside?' Thinking back, even at that point, she had sounded bored. Now that I'm telling you, it strikes me, there was a distinct note of bored fatigue in her voice.

Nevertheless, that is when I had walked down the tunnel of green. It was silent out there, the light dappled, bird songs a distant trill. I could hear my heart beat. And then suddenly, even while I searched, I realized absentmindedly, that the cobbled pathway under my feet had given way. I was walking on green grass now, freshly mown, my feet sinking into its dewy bank.

Finally, I found her after crossing the wooden Japanese bridge. She stood waiting in the radiance of the sun, slightly indistinct in all the luminosity. The golden haze has left tints on her cheekbones, entered the satiated afternoon of her eyes. There was a rose apple tree nearby, heavy with ripening fruit. The fruits made the bees buzz around us, a long-drawn drone. I flicked my hand, scared of the bristling bustle. But she merely said, 'Don't worry, they'll not bother us,' and I, quite quickly, eased myself into her calm, knowing confidence.

You want to know what we spoke about on that first day? Ah, quite natural. But please do not be surprised by my answer. For it was anything but normal. Like everything else about her, there was an innocent rebellion about it, as if she did not believe in conventional order, not because she disliked it, but because for a long, long time, she had lived in an order of her own. And now it was the only one that made any sense.

On that first day, she spoke about something that had happened bang in the middle of her life—with no preamble, with no pretense at helping me understand. Later, I would have to build bridges, little stepping stones in muddied waters to her past, the drawbridge that she let down over a placid canal, rife with blooming lotuses to her present.

But all that comes later, much later. First, we walked to the café which sits right on the brim of the garden, threatening to take the plunge anytime, like a suicidal man on the edge of a cliff. It was a nice enough café with quaint Georgian chairs and black and white pictures on its walls of a cemetery in the shade of deodar trees. If I was surprised by the café-owner's rather morbid taste in décor, I did not have time to comment, for Mithra started her story almost immediately—though I do not know if you can call those scratchy sentences a story. Yet, such was the magic of that afternoon and the languishing stupor of the chilled café that I seemed to understand, pictures forming in my mind with little prompting.

'Soon afterwards, I had a miscarriage. I lost so much blood that everyone thought I'd die.'

There was something about the way she rubbed her middle finger between her brows and tucked a tendril of hair behind her left ear before she spoke that told me that it had been a painful experience, that she was forcing herself to speak about it only because she wanted me to learn what she had learned from it. And later, when I heard her voice soften as she said 'We came to Singapore when my son was just shy of six months old', I realized how much she loves her children, and how much it had hurt to lose her first child.

And so, I built my own bridges.

Mithra, born into a house of prayers, growing up in their shadows like once, long ago, an ox[14] had shaded the infant Zarathustra when he was cast in the path of a raging horde. Before she really understood, she saw; and before she saw she heard. The deep glottal sound of the Avestan[15] words. Her father—standing by the window, in his white vest of the faithful, with its *giroban*, a little pocket for keeping good deeds—would say his prayers for what seemed like interminable hours, while life parted ways and thundered around them, leaving them in a little eye of calm.

But then came the full blaze of youth, that time of life when we know what we do not want long before we know what we want. And she rejected her father's prayers. She disliked the rituals, she told herself, 'The prayer tray[16] brought out every morning, what did those silver urns and lamps mean anyway?'

I cast a quick glance at her face. Is she embarrassed by the tale of her youth; the Prodigal Son brought back to the folds but not before he had lost his way?

But no, I realize she does not know how to hedge from the truth. Her faith teaches her not to. It is one of the good deeds she keeps in her giroban. In the face of conflict, she does not

---

[14] The ox is a part of the miraculous happenings that surround Zarathustra's birth. Repeatedly protected by animals of the wild and his essential righteousness, this recurring theme of his special relationship with animals underscores his protection of them from animal sacrifice.

[15] A sister language of Sanskrit, this is the language of Zarathustra's revelations. Zoroastrians chant their prayers in this old language which has survived from 1500 BCE, and though worshippers might not understand all the words, it is believed that it creates a strong effect on ether waves.

[16] Also known as Sace; usually made of silver, this ceremonial tray is an integral part of Parsi culture.

tiptoe around, but like Masaoka's horse plunges straight into the river.

'It wasn't easy. It never is. I made my own mistakes.'

She had left home and found herself caught in a maze. The middle of the maze is always the most difficult, you know. You are yet to find your path to the exit, and neither can you allow yourself the luxurious defeat of going back home. Every path led back to herself, it seemed there was no escaping the claustrophobia of being her.

It all ended with the painful miscarriage. Mesmerized, she watched the whirlpool gurgle out of the bath, clots of blood with which ran out her last hope of renewal. Exhausted, she lay inert, like moonlight on crumpled sheets, and around her voices murmured. Tortured hands craving for light, shifting shadows from a darkling plain.

All she needed to do was cross the bridge. The temptation to give up was strong.

Through her numbness, she could hear her father, 'It's all in your mind.[17] You know that, don't you? It's all in your mind. Push it away. Find the right path.'

---

[17] According to Zoroastrian belief, both Heaven and Hell are a state of mind, Heaven being the realm of the best mental existence in perpetual communion with Truth, and Hell the abode of the worst mind devoid of the Vision of Truth. Thus, 'He who is most good to the righteous, Be he a noble, or a peasant, or a dependent, He who zealously makes the good living creation flourish, He shall come to dwell with Truth in the realm of the Good Mind' (Gathas, *Yasna*, 33.3). Of Hell it says, 'These evil-doers, Who shall dwell in the abode of the Worst Mind, Who yearn for ill-gotten gain, and seethe from discontent, Who wantonly destroy life; Away from Thy Prophet's message, They shall not behold the Vision of Truth' (Gathas, *Yasna*, 32.13). Whether one resides in Heaven or Hell is a matter of choice dependent on whether one decides to embrace Asha i.e., Truth or Righteousness.

She had pushed away her father's ministering hand, told herself that she did not believe in these rituals. But her father had waited, waited every day for her return, eventually walking her back from the edge.

With him, she made a new beginning. They had visited a mountain resort to recuperate. There she had seen a mountain cemetery, in the shade of deodar trees, with few graves, where the worlds of life and death easily mingle. He had introduced her back to the white cotton sudreh of her faith, patiently taught her about their prayer tray—the long-necked silver *gulabaz* which held the wholeness of water, flowers and fruits with their message of immortality, the flame of Asha that rose in eternal truth of self-renewal[18].

She had looked up; outside her window were sun-drenched mountains, the shadow of sleeping deodars.

Through the slats
Of the outhouse door
Everest!

Clouds floated from the open palms of her hand. Her fingertips touched snow-covered mountain peaks on whose slopes slept an entire winter village. The waterfall that fell into

[18] On the prayer tray is present the seven elements—milk or yoghurt (Amesha Spenta Vahu Mano or the Good Mind), the flame (Amesha Spenta Asha or Righteousness and Piety), metal utensils (Amesha Spenta Khshathra or having dominance/sovereignty over one's life), water (Amesha Spenta Hauravat or seeking a holistic excellence in all one does), and flowers and fruits (Amesha Spenta Amertat or transcendence or immortality). The place of worship represents earth (Amesha Spenta Armaiti or serenity) and the practitioner Spenta Manyu. The Spenta Manyu is the beneficent spirit that allows one to realize one's higher calling, while possessing the Amesha Spenta qualities means being in harmony with God's work.

a pool of pine needles had entered the twinkling darkness of her hair.

I heard the next bit of her story a few days later, I think it was on our fourth of fifth meeting. In the meantime, we had talked about various things—how humans had once had the power to teleport themselves, how food was one of the ways to connect with the elements of the universe, how it was possible to enter the energies of another person. I was getting a bit impatient, I wanted something more concrete in my hands.

I have had enough of this kind of talk, I thought, I'm going to chase her into a cul-de-sac now.

Consequently, there was a new sharpness in my voice that day as I said, 'The path forked and you made the right choice—it sounds terribly predictable, you know!'

I look at her face to check her reaction but notice no resentment there. She stops for a moment to dwell on my question instead and I realize she accepts me at face value, without judgement or apprehension. That is yet another good deed she keeps in her giroban.

'But choice[19] is one thing that we always have. Free will is the special blessing of being human. Even now it's my choice if I want to talk to you or retire back into silence again.'

I try to feel miffed, wondering if she is trying to shake me off already. On top of it, at this point, she yawns hugely, making no attempt to hide it. Yet I feel no anger rise. There is a frank

---

[19] 'Hearken with your ears to these best counsels, Reflect upon them with illumined judgment. Let each one choose his creed with that freedom of choice each must have at great events. O ye, be awake to these, my announcements' (Gathas, *Yasna*, 30.2).

innocence about her, an involuntary honesty, like a child at play that makes anger impossible.

Today we have met in the bower, sitting under an archway of purple bougainvillea. There are flowers on her shirt too, daisies with upturned faces, red peonies. In the translucent darkness, it is impossible to tell where the red ends and the purple begins. I look at her—there is definitely a certain liminality about her, her eyes seem to hold more than one universe. It is where bees and flowers visit without fear the world of white cotton sudrehs and silver prayer trays. Mithra sits at the confluence.

'You know, that day at the resort when I looked out of my window at the deodar trees and mountain springs, I'd felt a sense of unity, a new power moving in me and I couldn't forget it easily.'

She had left for Igatpuri,[20] a Vipassana camp where she had heard it was taught how the human breath acted as a bridge between mind and body, could be used to understand both. And there, as she contemplated on the body in body, the feelings in feelings, consciousness in consciousness,[21] she had yet another experience.

While meditating in her room, she had felt the cells in her body vibrate. At first, it started at her finger tips and then spread till she felt her entire body, the dense formation of cells

---

[20] Dhamma Giri at Igatpuri, Maharashtra, India is one of the world's best-known centres for Vipassana Meditation as taught by S.N. Goenka in the tradition of the Burmese Theravadin monk, Sayagyi U Ba Khin.
[21] The Maha Sati Pattana Sutta, the sutta in Theravada Buddhism that explains the foundations of mindfulness states, 'This is the only way for monks, for the purification of beings, for the attainment of nibbana . . . contemplating the body in the body . . . feelings in feelings . . . consciousness in consciousness.'

that composed it, go into a state of intense vibration. It was a strange experience, as if the cells of her inner body were in a state of constant motion even while her outer body disintegrated. Flames rose from her outstretched palms, rising up, merging into the earth and sky.

'I'd run out of my room, screaming for help. I was scared.'

That experience changed her forever. Using her breath as a bridge, it put her in touch with the being within. And it also taught her the truth of what her father preached. That the seven elements inside her were also what composed the universe, that the world was nothing but her own self externalized. And the silver prayer tray with its seven elements was like the human breath, the conduit for connecting the inside with the outside, a symbol to remind her of her own immense power.

And now when she went back to the world of swaying deodar trees and mountain slopes over which clouds cast floating shadows, she saw nothing but herself. When she looked out of her window and saw the dappled sky, she knew it was her, stretching to the horizon in eternal protection. When she saw the cattle that grazed in the meadows, she saw in them nothing but herself—mild, sustaining, munificent.

It was almost as if all of creation was crying out in invitation:
Thereupon the Soul of Creation cried:
'In my woes I have obtained for help the feeble voice
of a humble man,
When I wished for a mighty overlord!
Whenever shall I get one to give me help with power
and with force?'[22]

Mithra had made her choice, found her own way out of the maze.

---

[22] Gathas, *Yasna*, 29.9.

A few weeks later I received an SOS call from her. She would soon be retiring into silence, and wanted to meet me one last time before she leaves.

This time we walk down the tunnel of green together. It is while we cross the little Japanese bridge that I ask her my first question.

'The worlds often look so similar. How do you choose between them?'

In reply, she smiles rather indulgently.

'No, but they are not! You need to look beyond the window dressing, the rows of flower pots, the sparrows on the flagstaff. That's when you will know the difference between body and body, thought and thought, consciousness and consciousness.'

It is from the Good Mind that discernment is born.[23] And so, from the eye of silence she makes her choice, and her path of freedom takes her to various doors. Instead of a normal school, she teaches at one based on a comprehensive curriculum at Kembangan which aims to connect a child with his higher self, to preserve in him what Wordsworth called his 'natural piety'. Rather than hear a god-man, she awakens through vipassana the giant in her own mind. With the world her home, she wakes up at dawn to pray that the world be restored to its natural state of benevolence. For she knows that all that makes an act moral is the intent.

We have crossed the bridge by now. She continues to speak of her prayers. In memory of her father, she has adopted the prayer tray. With infinite love she reveres rituals as much as she reveres her silence. She exists in unity with the universe, in a world where walls have fallen. It is a land of bridges here, timeless moments that carry in their heart reflections of perfection.

We stand by the winding canal. It is the twilight hour; luminosity embraces us like a warm golden fleece. A gold haze

---

[23] From the Good Mind is born discernment, 'Him with our good mind we seek to propitiate, Who gave us discernment through which we receive weal and woe.' Gathas, *Yasna*, 45.9.

tremors in the heart of the lotus, the same light that shines on
our inner truth. I ask her my second question,

'Why should we choose the Good Life? What benefit does
it bring us?'

Well, the smile gets a bit more indulgent. I fear that she
might just yawn again.

She tells me instead about how her father would stand by
the river bank and pray to the undying, shining, swift-horsed
sun.[24] Two pairs of hands stretch towards the setting sun, both
have known the tenderness of child rearing:

> *asato mā sadgamaya,*
> *tamaso mā jyotirgamaya,*
> *mṛtyormāmṛtaṃ gamaya*[25].
> From evil lead me to good,
> From darkness lead me to light,
> From death lead me to immortality.

She turns to me. I can see her eyes are getting distant, she
yearns to be away.

'The Good Life is its own vindication,'[26] she merely
mumbles.

---

[24] 'Hymn to the Sun' from the *Khorda Avesta*, the Parsi prayer book, describes
the sun thus.

[25] The Hindu Pavamana or purification mantra from the Upanishads.

[26] The choice of Righteousness is its own vindication, 'According to Thy
Faith, O Mazda, the choice of Righteousness is its own vindication, The
choice of evil, its own undoing; Hence do I seek and strive for the fellowship
of Good Thought, And renounce all association with the follower of Evil.'
Gathas, *Yasna*, 49.3.

It is while we stand under the heritage Saga tree, the tree that means different things in different cultures, and it spreads around us its coral reef of shiny red beads, that I ask her my final question. The sky is getting darker. It is one of those evenings in Singapore when an evening breeze blows through everything, demolishing walls, diminishing differences. The susurrus rising in the trees fuses with birdcalls and the buzzing of bees, creating an orchestra all its own.

'We've come all this way, Mithra. Where do we go from here?'

It is the time when day merges into night, life into death. The confluence is all there is.

'Nowhere. Just ease yourself into the flow[27]—like a fish enter the water without leaving a ripple, like an expert traveller enter the forest without moving a single blade of grass. End with Rumi like you had started and go back to the beginning.'

How does she know I intended to end with Rumi? I look at her. The evening light has left its tint on her cheekbones, has entered the fire in her eyes.

'The energies in the other realms are shifting,' she says. 'Surrender yourself to it.'

---

[27] The ancient Iranians believed truth was the way of the natural order, and by lending truth one's strength, one ensured the sustenance of the world in all its natural benevolence. And for one who attempted to do so, Ahura Mazda himself would be his counsel: 'For verily, through his Spirit of Righteousness and the Good Mind, He has ordained, That Perfection and Immortality shall be in His Dominion And vitality in perpetuity in His House! . . . To him, O Mazda, shalt Thou be a friend, brother, or even father!' Gathas, *Yasna*, 45.10–11.

I met last night in stealth with Wisdom's elder
begged him to divulge in full life's secrets
This he softly, softly whispered in my ear:
It must be seen, it can't be told, so hush!
Rumi, *Quatrain 1035*